# Th

*Welcome to t......................cy...*

With aristocra............................hree
men are set.............................eir
homes, no ma............................men
walk into their lives, they realize they have more to
contend with than they were expecting!

Introducing Toby Blythe, thirteenth Viscount of
Wishcliffe. When tragedy strikes his family, he
decides his accidental marriage in Vegas could
work in his favor upon his return to England...

Meet Lord Finn Clifford, Toby's best friend, healing
from a family betrayal. He must track down the
lost family heirlooms, but he may have just tracked
down his soul mate along the way!

Finally, we meet Max Blythe, Toby's illegitimate half
brother, who until now has been making his own
luck in life. Perhaps this time luck leaves him with
more than he bargained for...

Find out what happens in
Toby and Autumn's story
*Vegas Wedding to Forever*

and

Finn and Victoria's story
*The Second Chance Miracle*

Look out for the next book
Max and Lena's story
Coming soon!

Dear Reader,

Welcome back to Wishcliffe!

This time, we're not up at the stately home but instead in the village itself. We'll find ourselves at the antiques shop, the local pub—and in a small cottage by the sea, where a woman is trying to rebuild her life...with the help of a friend who doesn't realize how lost he is himself.

Finn and Victoria's story was always going to be an emotional one, but it surprised even me! Still, with jaunts around England and Paris hunting down antiques, and a chance to check in on Toby and Autumn from *Vegas Fling to Forever*, there's plenty of fun mixed in with the feels.

I hope you enjoy Finn and Victoria's journey together. Meanwhile, I'm off plotting a happy-ever-after for Toby's half brother, Max...

Love and antiques,

*Sophie* x

# Their Second Chance Miracle

—

## Sophie Pembroke

Recycling programs
for this product may
not exist in your area.

ISBN-13: 978-1-335-40703-0

Their Second Chance Miracle

Copyright © 2022 by Sophie Pembroke

This edition published by arrangement with Harlequin Books S.A.

For questions and comments about the quality of this book, please contact us at CustomerService@Harlequin.com.

Harlequin Enterprises ULC
22 Adelaide St. West, 41st Floor
Toronto, Ontario M5H 4E3, Canada
www.Harlequin.com

Printed in U.S.A.

**Sophie Pembroke** has been dreaming, reading and writing romance ever since she read her first Harlequin as part of her English literature degree at Lancaster University, so getting to write romantic fiction for a living really is a dream come true! Born in Abu Dhabi, Sophie grew up in Wales and now lives in a little Hertfordshire market town with her scientist husband, her incredibly imaginative and creative daughter, and her adventurous, adorable little boy. In Sophie's world, happy *is* forever after, everything stops for tea and there's always time for one more page...

### Books by Sophie Pembroke

### Harlequin Romance

#### *The Heirs of Wishcliffe*

*Vegas Wedding to Forever*

#### *Cinderellas in the Spotlight*

*Awakening His Shy Cinderella*
*A Midnight Kiss to Seal the Deal*

#### *A Fairytale Summer!*

*Italian Escape with Her Fake Fiancé*

*Pregnant on the Earl's Doorstep*
*Snowbound with the Heir*
*Second Chance for the Single Mom*
*The Princess and the Rebel Billionaire*

Visit the Author Profile page
at Harlequin.com for more titles.

For everyone who has lost someone they love over the last couple of years.

But most especially, in memory of Eden Anna.

## Praise for
## Sophie Pembroke

"An emotionally satisfying contemporary romance full of hope and heart, *Second Chance for the Single Mom* is the latest spellbinding tale from Sophie Pembroke's very gifted pen. A poignant and feel-good tale that touches the heart and lifts the spirits."

—*Goodreads*

# CHAPTER ONE

IT HAD BEEN a long time since Finn Clifford last walked the cobbled streets of Wishcliffe village on a mission, but he had one now. One final step towards the goal that had driven him for the last decade.

Growing up at Clifford House, less than a mile away, his usual goals in Wishcliffe had to do with hanging out with his best friend Toby Blythe and trying to obtain illegal pints at the King's Arms pub. But he was an adult now—a thirty-something even, as Toby, now his business partner, kept reminding him with a smirk. He had a purpose in life. He was a successful businessman, a force to be reckoned with, a world away from the boy he had been…

But he still winced when he saw the ancient bent form of John Yarrow sitting on his usual bench outside the King's Arms, smoking his pipe.

'Finn Clifford, as I live and breathe,' John called out across the street, his breath misting in the cold air. 'Been a while. Not looking for mischief, I hope?'

'No mischief, sir,' Finn called back. 'I'm on a mission.'

'Are you now?' John's gaze was assessing. 'Sounds like it's going to get you into trouble.'

'Probably,' Finn admitted. 'But it'll be worth it.'

'Hmm.' John sucked on his pipe, then nodded. 'Get on with it, then.'

Finn picked up his pace.

The weak January sun had barely managed to make it above the rooftops of the cotton-candy-coloured cottages that lined the side streets leading down to the sea. In summer, the village would be bustling with locals, tourists and day-trippers from the surrounding towns, all looking for the coastal charm Wishcliffe provided in spades. But today the high street was empty, a number of the shops not even open for the day.

The shop he wanted was, though. From the cross at the centre of the village, where High Street and Water Street met, Finn could see the yellow glow of the lamps in the window and the rusting metal shop sign swaying in the breeze from the sea beyond.

He stalled for a moment, breathing in the salt air until his lungs felt cold. Part of him—not a small part either—wanted to turn around and head back to the tiny car park by the chapel where he'd left his car. But that wouldn't be in keeping with his mission. And he'd come too far over the last few years to give up now, when he was so close.

This was the final stage of a decade-long plan of revenge. He couldn't stop now, even if he wanted to.

Besides, the worst she could say was no, right?

Resolved, Finn headed down Water Street and pushed open the door to Wishcliffe Antiques and Collectibles without even pausing to glance through the window first.

Victoria looked up as the bell over the door jingled, and Finn felt a jolt as his heart jumped into his throat. In the yellowing light of the coloured glass lampshades dotted on the shelves around her, she appeared more beautiful than ever.

Her silky dark hair was caught up in a simple ponytail at the base of her neck, and her severe black jacket and top did nothing to accentuate the gorgeous figure he knew was hidden underneath. She was thinner than he remembered, her eyes a little large in her face, the shadows under them not quite hidden by make-up. But she'd never looked more beautiful to him.

*Stop staring,* he told himself fiercely. *She's Barnaby's. She'll always be Barnaby's.*

And because of that he would only ever be able to admire her from a distance, never letting her know how perfect he thought she was. He'd resigned himself to that years ago, that first summer Toby's older brother Barnaby had brought her home to Wishcliffe after they met at university.

He'd fallen in love—or at least lust—on the spot. And known in that same instance that he could never do anything about it—least of all let Victoria know how he felt. So he hadn't. Not in all the fifteen years that had followed. Barnaby had been like a big brother to Finn too. He would never do anything to betray that.

Not even now he was gone.

'Finn!' Victoria's smile looked forced, but that wasn't really a surprise. 'How lovely. What can I do for you?'

That was her hostess voice, Finn recognised. The one she'd used as the lady of the manor, Viscountess Wishcliffe, before she was widowed. Before she'd been replaced last September, when Toby came home to inherit his older brother's title as Viscount, and brought his new American bride, Autumn, with him.

She'd never used that tone with him, though. He'd always been family, before now.

'Toby told me you were working here now,' he said, not answering her question. Not yet. 'I had to see it for myself to believe it.'

Victoria bristled at that. 'I have a degree in art history and a master's in art business, plus several years' experience of working at auction houses. What's so incredible about me working at an antiques shop?'

He'd set them off on the wrong foot already, which was sort of par for the course for him with Victoria. He'd never been able to keep his foot out of his mouth around her.

'I'd forgotten about you working up in town.' He hadn't. Finn didn't think he'd forgotten anything about Victoria from the moment they'd met.

She'd commuted into London from Wishcliffe, where she was already living with

Barnaby, planning their grand wedding, and only quit after their son, Harry, was born. She'd planned to go back, he knew, but then Toby and Barnaby's father died and Barnaby took up the title, and she'd had more than enough to do as Viscountess, keeping Wishcliffe from going under.

But that was Toby and Autumn's job now, and here Victoria was. Getting back to her roots.

'I wasn't suggesting you weren't qualified to be here,' he said when she stayed silent. 'I'd have thought you were over-qualified, if anything.'

'I've been out of the antiques world a long time.' She sounded faintly mollified. 'This seemed like a good way to ease myself in, and Joanne needed the help in the shop, so it worked out for both of us.'

'That's…good.' Finn perched himself on the corner of an old oak sideboard, until Victoria glared at him and he slid off again, hands in his pockets. 'Actually, it's antiques I came to speak to you about.'

Her eyebrows jumped at that, surprise obvious on her face. 'Antiques? I've seen your London flat, Finn. There's not a thing older than last year in the whole place.'

A slight exaggeration, but he had to admit that he favoured a more modern aesthetic in his London home. 'Ah, but this isn't for the flat. It's for Clifford House.'

Victoria's eyes widened as she leant forward across the desk. 'You really did it then? You bought back Clifford House?'

Nobody had thought he could, not even his closest friends, not really. But Clifford House was his by rights—by birth, by history, by inheritance. It had been passed down to the eldest son in the Clifford line for so many generations that they'd run out of room on the family tree. It was the place he'd been born, the place he'd grown up, the place that he'd always known would come to him.

The last place he'd seen his mother alive. The only place he had happy childhood memories with her.

Clifford House belonged to him, and he belonged to it. And now, finally, that was official in the eyes of the law again.

Pride filled him as he nodded. 'I really did.' It had taken him a decade to earn the money and orchestrate the sale. Ten years since the day he'd learned that his own father had sold his heritage, his home, purely to keep it from ever falling into Finn's hands.

Not just Clifford House itself, or the grounds that surrounded it, but every heirloom, every keepsake, every stick of furniture that went with it. 'But that's just the start.'

Because if his father's aim had been to stop Finn from ever being Lord at Clifford House after his death, then he had failed. And Finn had every intention of rubbing his nose in that failure.

'The start?' Victoria asked. 'What's next?'

'Next, I have to buy back all the heirlooms and antiques to fill the place. And that's where you come in.'

Victoria stared at Finn, taking in the smirk on his lips and the fire in his eyes.

Of course. He'd only come to find her because he needed her help. That made sense.

Or maybe Toby had put him up to it—had him come up with a pity job to keep Poor Victoria busy now she'd handed the estate over to him and Autumn. Never mind that she'd *wanted* to leave.

She'd stayed on at Wishcliffe for a full year after the horrific sailing accident that took her husband and son from her. She'd lived in that big house full of all its memories, and she'd followed the plans that she and Barnaby had made together, to try and make the estate solvent. She'd given Toby the time he needed to tie up his business loose ends—and to get to a mental place where he was ready to take on the job as Viscount, something he'd never thought would fall to him.

Victoria had done everything she could and then she'd stepped back gracefully to let Autumn take her rightful place as Viscountess, while she'd helped and supported her from the sidelines. And when they were settled up at Wishcliffe House she'd moved out—even if it was only as far as her little cottage on the outskirts of the village, by the sea. She'd found herself a new job. She'd stepped into a new life. A quieter, safer, softer life than the one she'd thought she'd be living with Barnaby and Harry, but *her* life all the same.

She'd done everything properly. Everything right. Thinking of others all the way.

But that wasn't enough, apparently. Toby and Autumn still insisted on dragging her back to the main house for dinner every week, still fretted that she wasn't happy, that she needed more in her life. More people, more adventure, more challenge.

What none of them seemed to understand was that she'd *had* all that. She'd had true love, the fairy-tale prince—well, viscount in her case—the perfect family, the happily-ever-after.

It just seemed that 'ever after' didn't last as long as it used to, that was all.

Victoria knew that her life had been blessed—from the moment she'd met Barnaby until the moment she'd lost him and their son at sea. She'd had all her good fortune and used it up fast. All she hoped for now was a quiet, settled, content existence, doing things she was good at. Was that so much to ask?

Apparently so, because now here was Finn, with a huge project that he just *had* to have her help for—as if there weren't a hundred antiques dealers in London who would jump at the chance to take it on.

'Toby put you up to this, didn't he?' she said accusingly.

Finn looked honestly taken aback. 'No. I haven't actually spoken to him about it yet—he's meeting me at Clifford House later. I wanted to get you on board first.'

'You really expect me to believe that after a year away you've come back completely without prompting to ask me to take on your little revenge shopping trip?'

'It's not a revenge shopping trip,' Finn said

with distaste. Victoria raised her eyebrows. 'Fine, it is. But can we at least call it something else? Like a Heritage Restoration Project?'

He didn't mention the year away. Victoria wasn't surprised. He wasn't the only friend who'd dropped out of her life once her circumstances changed. People weren't sure how to deal with a thirty-three-year-old widow who'd lost not just her husband but her only child as well. It was too sad for them, so they stayed away.

Joanne, who owned the antiques shop, had helped her come to terms with that. She'd lost her husband in her late forties and moved to Wishcliffe to get away from the pitying looks and the blind date set-ups.

*'People start to panic that you'll be on your own, you see,'* she'd said when Victoria had wandered in one day, three months after the funeral, looking for a distraction. *'You're an aberration. So they try to fix you. To find you a new life, before you've finished saying goodbye to your old one. Either that or they stay away, like what happened to you might be catching. They're scared is all, and they're thinking of themselves instead of you. You*

*take your time, do what you need to do, and ignore all the rest, okay?'*

Joanne had become a friend, long before she'd been her boss. Victoria credited her with helping her find her feet. Her own path towards what she wanted the rest of her life to be.

Peaceful mostly, she'd decided.

Finn Clifford's life, Victoria knew, was anything but peaceful.

Even before his father had upped and sold Clifford House and all its contents, just to stop it falling into the hands of a son he regularly described as 'degenerate', the people of Wishcliffe and the surrounding area had all known of the drama playing out in the family. From Finn's mother walking out when he was a child—only to die a year later in a car crash with her lover—to the knockdown, drag-out fights between father and son that had required the police to be called more than once, Finn's life was definitely dramatic.

And that was something that Victoria wanted no part of.

'It'll be fun,' he cajoled, obviously sensing he was about to get rejected. 'Like a treasure hunt. That's what we should call it! My Heritage Treasure Hunt. Buying back all the things my father sold and shoving our successes in his face. It'll be great!'

'For you, maybe.' Victoria shook her head. 'Do you even realise what you're asking, Finn? It'll be months of research, travel, work… I'm not up for that. And besides, I don't think this focus on revenge is good for you. You've bought the house. Isn't that enough?'

His whole adult life, that was what he'd been focused on, as far as Victoria could see. Being successful enough, earning enough, to buy back Clifford House after his father sold it when Finn was away at Oxford, in his last year of university.

And now he'd done it. Shouldn't that be enough?

'No,' Finn said, his voice cold. 'It's not enough. But I need your help for the rest. Please, Victoria.'

The please almost broke her. That and the idea of being needed again. Having a purpose beyond living out her quiet, safe days.

But that wasn't her plan for her future.

'I'm sorry, Finn. I can't.' She shrugged apologetically. 'I have obligations here, working for Joanne, apart from anything else. I can't just up and run away on a treasure hunt with you.'

Even if a part of her wanted to. A small, secret part of her that had been quiet for such a long time, and was now stirring again at the thought of a new adventure.

His disappointment was clear on his face, but he didn't press her any further.

'I understand.' Finn reached across the counter to place a palm against her shoulder. 'Take care of yourself, Victoria. And let me know if you change your mind.' He turned and walked away, back out into Water Street, heading for the cross.

'I won't,' she whispered to herself as the door closed behind him.


'I love what you haven't done with the place, Finn.'

Finn started as his best friend's voice echoed through the empty rooms of Clifford House. Turning away from the window, he gave Toby a wry smile as he joined him in what had always been the ballroom, a vast open space with wooden floors and huge windows leading out onto the terrace. Finn vaguely remembered a ball being held there once, but that must have been long before his mother had left, and he didn't have so many memories left from that time. Just the impression of swirling dresses and music and staying up past his bedtime.

Most of his memories of Clifford House weren't the happiest. But they were his, just like the house. And some of them, the earliest ones…

Sitting with his mother in her favourite garden, making up fairy tales together. Baking mince pies with her at Christmas. Curling up beside the fire after playing in the snow while she made him hot chocolate, and knowing that he was loved.

Those memories were what he forced himself to remember when he looked around Clifford House now. Not the others. *They* were the reason this place mattered.

Something else he wouldn't let his father take away from him.

'Well, you wanted to see it.' Finn spread his arms wide to encompass the vast emptiness of the old Georgian-style manor house. 'Here it is.'

'Not *quite* as I remember it,' Toby observed. 'I seem to remember there being, oh, furniture, maybe?'

'I'm working on it. Come on, I've got the kitchen up and running at least.'

He led Toby through the warren of corridors to the kitchen, ignoring the empty space where the old farmhouse table used to sit and directing him to one of the folding chairs beside a rickety picnic table instead. 'Coffee? Or beer?'

'Coffee's fine,' Toby replied, gazing around at the space. 'So, what's first on your agenda here?'

Finn flipped on the kettle. He really needed to get a proper coffee-maker set up in here. Coffee, then furniture, that was the actual plan—but probably not what Toby was asking.

'That depends,' he said. 'I got lucky in that the most recent owners only got as far as making the place good and painting it all white before they ran out of funds and had to sell. Apparently this place has been a money pit for at least three other families since my father sold it.'

'So you've got a blank canvas. You can really make this place your own.' Toby sounded approving of that—maybe even a little jealous, Finn thought. 'What I wouldn't give sometimes to start over at Wishcliffe. I think there are spiders' webs in some of the corners that are older than me.'

'You don't mean that.' For Finn, Wishcliffe House had always been the perfect beacon of cosiness and welcoming warmth. With its roaring fire in the winter, apple cider fresh from the orchard and warm biscuits just out of the oven, it was the only place Finn had wanted to spend his school holidays after his mother was gone. Even when Clifford House had been filled with furniture, it had never been welcoming to him without her there. 'Besides, I refuse to believe that Mrs Heath would suffer a spider to live on her watch.'

'True.' Toby gave a half smile at the reminder of his terrifyingly efficient housekeeper. 'Still, do you know there's not a single piece of furniture or decoration in that place that Autumn and I picked out ourselves? It's all heirlooms. Whereas here…' He trailed off, perhaps realising that he was treading on uncomfortable ground.

'Here, my father sold all our family heirlooms, just so they'd never be mine,' Finn said. 'But the joke's on him, because I'm going to buy them all back.'

Toby blinked. 'What? All of them? Isn't that a little…ambitious?'

Finn had a strong suspicion that 'ambitious' wasn't his friend's first choice of word to finish that sentence. 'Fine. Maybe not all of them. But the important ones I want to track down and buy back. As for the rest of the house, I plan to find pieces as close as possible to the ones that were here before. I'm going to put this place back the way it was before my father lost his mind.' And then he would bring the old man back to Clifford House and show him that he'd lost. That Finn had got everything he'd tried to deny him and there wasn't a damn thing he could do about it.

Rubbing a hand over his forehead, Toby gave Finn a concerned look. 'You don't think that just buying back the house was enough? I mean, that's what you were always focused on. What you've been working for all these years. Can't you, I don't know, just enjoy it?'

It hadn't been enough for Lord Clifford to make his only son's life miserable. He'd had to take away everything that was his by rights. To badmouth him to the whole of society. And to do it just as Finn had been poised to graduate, to step out into the world of work and make a life for himself. While the parents and families of his fellow students had been setting up opportunities for them, introducing them to people they needed to know, or at least helping them with job applications and housing them in the meantime, Lord Clifford had been systematically undermining Finn's attempts to make his way in the world.

Every interview Finn had attended after Oxford had been met by a knowing look from someone on the other side of the desk—someone who knew his father or had heard the rumours. Finn Clifford was unreliable, a degenerate, a failure. It was a large part of why Finn had persuaded Toby that they should set up their own business—and then let Toby be the public face of the company, at least to start with.

His father had tried to ruin his whole life.

So, no. It wasn't enough just to have the house back, even though that alone was a huge measure of his success. He had to *show* his father how utterly he'd undone everything Lord Clifford had strived to achieve. Turn back the clock to before his mother had left, to when Clifford House had actually felt like home.

Finn shook his head. 'It's not enough, Toby. You know it isn't. You know what my father did. What he is. It's not enough to have the house. I've got to beat him *completely,* or he'll always feel like he's won.'

'Right.' Toby sighed. 'Okay, well, if we're doing this, we're going to need help.'

'We?'

Toby shrugged. 'You're my best friend. You might sound kind of obsessive crazy right now, but if you didn't turn your back on me when I accidentally got married to a woman I didn't know in Vegas, I'm not abandoning you now.'

'And look how well that Vegas thing worked out for you and Autumn,' Finn pointed out. Not only were they still married, but they were planning a spring ceremony and party to celebrate it with all their friends in Wishcliffe. 'Maybe this will be more successful than you think.'

'Maybe.' Toby didn't sound convinced. 'But you're still going to need more help than me—I don't know the first thing about antiques.' Enlightenment hit him, and Finn watched as Toby caught up to where Finn had been since the moment he'd walked into his new old property and realised what his next steps needed to be. 'Victoria! She's the antiques expert. And honestly, I've been a bit worried about her lately. I know she says she likes working at the shop, but she's used to running a whole *estate*. She's got to be bored. And I don't want her to just give up on life the way my mother did when Dad died. This could be the perfect project to get her engaged again!'

'She said no,' Finn said, and watched as Toby's excitement deflated.

'You already spoke to her?'

Finn nodded. 'This morning. She's not interested.'

Toby's face darkened. 'Because she's not interested in *anything* any more. Autumn keeps trying to get her involved with the planning for our wedding celebration, and I've been asking her about playing a part in some of the new projects up on the estate, but she keeps making excuses not to get involved.'

Finn suspected that probably had more to do with Victoria wanting to draw a line between the life she'd lost and the one she was living, but he could see how worried Toby was about her, so he didn't say so.

'What do you think I should do, then?'

'Keep at her,' Toby said. 'Don't let her just give up on everything that used to matter to her. Okay? Keep asking until she says yes.'

Finn had always believed that when a lady

said no he should accept that and walk away. But in this case he could almost see Toby's point. Victoria was pulling away from the people who loved her right when she needed them most. And the life she was building for herself, alone…was it one she really wanted? Or the only thing she thought was open to her?

If Victoria had turned him down not because she didn't want to help but because she thought that was what she should do as a widowed woman, then he at least had to give her a nudge, didn't he?

Nothing at all to do with the fact that just the idea of spending more time with her made him smile.

'I'll see what I can do,' Finn said. 'First, do you have a number for Joanne Soames?'

# CHAPTER TWO

VICTORIA DIDN'T BOTHER with the front door. She might not know Clifford House the way she knew Wishcliffe, but she knew Finn wouldn't be hanging around in the oversized entrance hall. So she skirted the edge of the driveway and slammed open the back door to the kitchen instead.

Finn, sitting in a camping chair, put down his coffee cup on the blue plastic picnic table beside him. 'Hello, Victoria. This is a—'

'You called my boss.' The fury that had started to rise in her the moment Joanne had told her was reaching fever-pitch. 'I told you no, and you ignored me. You went over my head and called my boss and sweet talked her instead.'

'Well, I knew sweet talk never works on you.' Finn stood and headed to the mostly bare kitchen counter. 'Coffee?'

'You couldn't accept that *I* have the final say in my life?' Victoria asked, before adding, 'And yes to coffee.' It had been a long day, after all. Mostly because of the man holding the jar of instant coffee.

He might have left the antiques shop that morning without a fuss, but his request had stayed in her head long past lunchtime. And when Joanne had arrived to help close up at the end of the day and announced that she'd had a very interesting phone call, Victoria had known she wasn't done with Finn just yet.

'You absolutely do have the final say in your life.' Finn handed her the coffee and motioned to the second camping chair, which was a total mismatch for the first in colour and style. 'I just wanted to make sure you made that decision for yourself, and not for other people.'

'Other people like, say, you?' Victoria stayed standing when he sat down again, taking advantage of being taller than him for once as she looked down at him.

He chuckled at that, which wasn't what she'd been aiming for. He should be feeling guilty for trying to manipulate her, not amused.

'You said you couldn't help because you had to work at the shop for Joanne. So I spoke to Joanne.' Finn shrugged. 'If you don't want to help me because you genuinely don't want to help me, that's fine. I'm sure I can find someone else who will. But if you're saying no because you think you shouldn't for some reason—because of your obligations to Joanne, or because, well, I don't know, some other stupid reason like what you think a widow's life has to look like—then I have to at least give you all the information, and an opportunity to change your mind.'

He looked up at her with a smile so persuasive that it should have been illegal, and Victoria gave up and dropped into the chair beside him.

*What you think a widow's life has to look like.*

*Was* that what she was doing?

She'd been determined not to, but now she looked at the life she was building she had to admit she'd gone for safe over fun, for quiet over passion. Because fun and passion were what she'd had with Barnaby, and Barnaby was gone.

'Joanne said you offered to pay for my time while I was working for you, so she could hire someone else to help in the shop if she needed to, when I was away.' Joanne had also told her to think about why she was saying no.

*'Be honest with yourself. Working here at my little shop was only ever going to be your first step back to a new career, wasn't it?'*

Because that was what she'd told everyone when she'd taken the job. That it was her first step. She just hadn't actually gone as far as to imagine taking any future steps at all.

'It's only fair, after all,' Finn said. 'If you're working for me, I pay for your services. Just like I would anyone else. I wasn't asking for a favour.'

'Right.' But what *was* he asking for, exactly? 'You said you wanted to buy back some heirlooms, find some antiques for this place. How many are we talking about?'

Finn's smile turned wry as he got to his feet. 'Let me give you the tour.' He held out a hand and pulled her out of her own chair. 'Starting here in the kitchen, where we need, well, everything, as you can see.'

'Like a kitchen table and chairs, that sort of thing?' That should be easy enough to source, at least.

'Exactly. Just like there used to be in here.' He led her out into the hallway and through to what must be a beautiful drawing room—when it wasn't cold and empty. 'And in here they had matching Queen Anne chairs, plus an upholstered chaise longue in a duck egg Chinese design, as far as I can tell from the photos. I'm not sure how easy they'll be to come by. And through here—'

'Wait!' Victoria called out, stopping him before he could whirlwind her into the next empty, soulless room. 'You want to recreate this place exactly as it was when your parents lived here?'

He stared at her blankly. 'Well, yes. Of course. Isn't that what I told you this morning?'

'I thought…well, I suppose I thought you wanted help finding antiques that would suit the place.' She stared around at the white walls and the curtainless windows. Surely it couldn't be healthy, recreating the home she knew he'd hated growing up in.

The summer she'd met Finn, when he was sixteen and she was eighteen, he'd spent more time at Wishcliffe House than his own—and, according to Barnaby, it had been that way since Toby and he were kids. Ever since Finn's mother had left, and his father started drinking.

'I just don't understand why,' she said help-
lessly.

'Because I need my father to know that I
won in the end. And this is how I'm going to
do it.' Finn placed a hand on the doorframe.
'I'm going to show him that everything he
tried to take away from me I won back in
the end.'

Yeah, this definitely wasn't healthy. 'You
don't think that, say, living a full and meaningful life of your own might do that better?
People matter more than things, Finn.'

'Not to my father, they don't,' he said
wryly. 'I could be President of the Universe,
happily married with a whole platoon of kids,
and I'd still be his useless, degenerate son to
him. This place—our heritage—is the only
thing that's ever meant a damn to him. So
that's what I have to use.'

'Why?' she asked again, uncertain whether
she meant *Why do it?* or *Why does he hate
you so much?*

She wasn't entirely sure which one he answered either, when he said, 'If I figure it out
I'll let you know. So, will you help me?'

This time Victoria didn't glance around at
the empty spaces, the rooms waiting to be
filled, the blank walls crying out for pictures.

Instead, she looked at Finn—really looked at him, for the first time since he'd walked into Joanne's antique shop that morning.

What she saw there reminded her of her own mirror, not so very long ago. The desperate search for something to make sense of the world.

He was going about it the wrong way, of course. If she'd learned anything in the last thirty-three years it was that acquiring more stuff never led to happiness—acquiring more people, more love, was the only way she'd ever found to do that.

But if this was what he believed he needed… she could help him. And she could be a friend when he realised that it wasn't enough. Because Finn really looked like he needed a friend right then.

She moistened her lips, weighing her words in her head before she spoke. 'I'll help you. But I'll do it my way, on my terms.'

Finn smiled, slow and warm. 'Whatever you need, Victoria.'

She was going to help him. Which meant he might actually be able to pull this whole scheme off, after all. Relief mixed with joy inside him. 'So, where do we start?'

Victoria looked as surprised as he was that she'd said yes. 'Uh… I guess we finish the tour of the house?'

'The rooms all look pretty much like this one,' Finn admitted. 'Soulless and white. But I guess you need to get an idea of the scale of the problem, so…come on.'

It felt so strange, touring the empty rooms of his childhood home with his teenage crush at his side. Victoria paid attention to everything, asking questions about his memories of what each room had been like and taking notes in a small book she pulled from her handbag.

'You said you have photos?' she asked as they reached the bedrooms.

Finn nodded. 'Not of every room, but most. It should get us close enough. I've got a designer working on finding matches for the wallpaper, curtains and the like.'

'Right.' She still sounded perturbed at his plan. Finn could understand that. It wasn't as if he was under the impression that this was a totally *normal* thing to do.

But it was what he needed—what his father needed to see for him to understand. To know that he hadn't beaten Finn, hadn't destroyed him, despite all his best efforts.

Once he'd done this, Finn would be free of his father, his past, for ever. *Then* he could move on with his life. But not before.

'Come on.' He led her into the next room, a smaller corner space with large windows on two sides. Even though it, like all the other rooms, was painted plain white, in his memory it was a sunny yellow, with a rocking chair in the bay window where his mother used to sit and sing to him. 'This was my nursery.'

'It's a lovely room.' The words sounded strained, and he glanced over to find her face tense and drawn.

Of course. He'd been so caught up in his own past he'd forgotten for a moment about hers.

She'd lost her child. Her son.

In Finn's memory, Harry had been a vibrant child—always in motion, always smiling and laughing. Losing her husband must have been heart-breaking. But losing her child…

Finn didn't know how Victoria still got out of bed every morning.

'Let's head back down to the kitchen.' He guided her out of the room and towards the stairs, and she let him. 'It's warmer there, for a start—the central heating is something else that's on my list to get someone out here to look at.' But the kitchen had the old Aga in it, always lit and always warm, just like he remembered from his childhood.

There were *some* good memories associated with this place, he'd come to realise since moving back. They just tended to get lost in the weight of all the bad ones.

'So, how is this going to work?' Finn asked as he put the kettle on for another round of hot drinks.

'As my employer, I was sort of expecting you to tell me that.' Victoria, settled back into one of the camping chairs, looked more herself again, he was relieved to see.

'Yeah, but out of the two of us, you're the only one who knows what they're doing.'

She laughed at that, and he tried not to grin with pride at having achieved it, the way he would have done at sixteen, trying to impress the girl he had a crush on.

Not much had changed in the last fifteen years, he had to admit.

'Well, I think we need to focus in on what you *really* want to achieve here.' She took her mug from him, and Finn sat down beside her to listen. 'I mean, this place is enormous, Finn. If you really wanted to refurnish it exactly as it was when you were growing up, it could take years. Longer, if you wanted exact matches for all of the pieces. The antiques market is buoyant, but there are still some pieces that don't come up—or not for the price you'd be willing to pay.'

'I'll pay anything,' he replied automatically. Buying Clifford House might have dented his savings, but it hadn't depleted them. The business was doing well, and he'd been working towards this for years. He wasn't worried about the money.

'You say that now,' Victoria said wryly. 'Wait until the first time I tell you you're going to have to pay the equivalent of two month's rent for a dining room chair—and you need six of them.'

Finn shook his head. 'I don't care. I'll pay it.'

'You shouldn't.' She gave him an assessing look. 'Finn, the point about antiques isn't just owning them for the sake of it, or because they're old and expensive. You're buying a piece of heritage. A place in history.' Her eyes lit up as she spoke and Finn knew this really mattered to her, so he listened a little harder—and tried not to get distracted by how beautiful she looked when she cared about something. 'Plus a lot of the pieces your father sold won't be up for sale again—at any price, possibly—even if I could track them all down. I think a couple of the paintings went to museums, for instance, if I'm remembering right.'

'Okay, so how would *you* recommend we go about this?' he asked. 'You know what I'm trying to achieve here, and why. How do I do it?'

She looked thoughtful for a moment, staring down at the open notebook on her lap, where she'd been jotting notes throughout their tour. 'I think you need to choose the pieces that really matter—a handful of the real heirlooms, the ones you want back. I'll work on tracking those down and see how many of them we can buy back.'

'Sounds good so far.' He'd never really imagined—outside of daydreams—that he'd be able to get *everything* back. But there were pieces he knew beyond doubt he had to have to complete his plan. The mantel clock given to his ancestor by a member of a royal family— or possibly *the* royal family. The writing desk his mother had brought with her when she'd married his father. A painting of his grand-mother. That sort of thing. 'Then what?'

'For the rest of the rooms…let's choose the ones that will have the most impact and start there, trying to replace the furnishings with as close a match as we can get. But for things like the third guest bedroom… Finn, you might just have to accept that we'll find something lovely to suit the space, but it might not be exactly the same.'

He nodded. 'I can do that. I mean, there are some rooms that I don't even have reference photos for—we were always going to have to guess there. And as long as every room is furnished in a similar style, the impact should be the same.'

'Exactly!' Victoria beamed at him, the light in her eyes a full-on blaze now. 'In that case… I think we can do this. Do you want to give me the photos and other reference mate-rial now, and I can get started while I'm work-ing at the shop tomorrow? From what you've said, I've already got a few ideas on places we can try, people to speak to, that sort of thing.'

'I'll get them now.' She looked so alive, so engaged by the challenge. Almost like she had before she'd lost everything. Toby had been right; she needed this, even if she hadn't known it.

And Finn couldn't help but feel happy that he'd been the one to give it to her.

'Thank you, Victoria. For helping me with this.'

Her smile warmed places inside him he'd forgotten even existed. 'We'll see if you're still thanking me when I've spent all your money on antique china,' she said.

Finn laughed, and went to fetch the file.

Going through Finn's research at the shop the next day, Victoria realised she might have underestimated the amount of work that was going to be involved in this project.

Oh, she'd known it would be a big job, no doubt about that. But some of the pieces Lord Clifford had sold off were unique, and plenty of the others were incredibly rare. The specific items Finn wanted weren't things she was likely to stumble over at an antiques market or dusty old curios shop in some little town.

She was separating the items in his file into three stacks based on the likelihood of being able to buy them back, buy something similar or find something from vaguely the same period when the Bakelite rotary dial phone beside the till rang.

'Wishcliffe Antiques,' she said, absently filing Finn's mother's china set under 'buy something similar'. 'How can I help you?'

'You already are.' Finn's voice was warm and friendly in her ear, and she smiled despite herself. 'Just calling to see how you're getting on with the files. If there's anything else you need, that sort of thing.'

Victoria surveyed the towering piles of paper. 'I think I've got plenty to be going on with for now, thanks. But if you want to come over later this evening we can discuss our next moves?'

'Sounds good,' Finn said. 'Shall I bring anything?'

'Coffee is always appreciated. See you later.'

She hung up and returned her attention to the files—only for a breeze from the door to send half of them skittering across the floor.

'Sorry! Sorry,' Joanne said as she dropped to her knees to help collect them up again, almost spilling the two takeaway coffees she was carrying over all of them.

Victoria swept in and took the travel mugs from her and placed them safely on the desk.

'Don't worry, I've got a system. But thank you for the coffee.'

Joanne stepped back, hands on her hips, and eyed Victoria's carefully organised stacks as she reassembled them. 'You know, when Finn Clifford called and asked to borrow you for a project, I kind of assumed that was just an excuse for him to get you alone and ask you out.'

Finn? Ask her out? A laugh exploded from Victoria's mouth at the very idea. 'No, this is an actual work project.'

'Well, I can see that now.' Joanne took her coffee and perched safely out of the way on a vintage school desk. 'What's he got you doing?'

'Buying back or replacing most of the contents of Clifford House.'

Joanna gave a low whistle. '*That* is a project. Shame.'

'Why's it a shame?' Victoria asked, peering at her boss over the top of a photo of the main hallway during some sort of party.

'Because if he *was* looking for an excuse to ask you out, you have to admit he's a bit of a hottie.'

Victoria laughed again at that, even if it didn't feel quite so amusing. 'I've known Finn since he was sixteen. He's like a little brother to me. Well, maybe not brother. Brother's best friend, I guess.'

Because while Toby had always been the sibling she'd never had and always wanted, from the moment they'd met Finn was more aloof, apart, in some ways. For all that he'd been around Wishcliffe House as much as the Blythe brothers, he'd always been on the edges of the action. Victoria supposed that was why they'd bonded at first—both outsiders to this strange family, both trying to find their place.

Finn had been the one to explain the vagaries of Wishcliffe to her—all the little oddities that seemed normal to Barnaby and Toby because they'd grown up with them, but made no sense at all to her that first summer. The one she'd exchanged amused looks with when any of the Blythes did something particularly Blythe-like.

'Brother's best friend is *definitely* not a brother.' Joanne gave her an assessing look. 'You're absolutely sure he's not working up to asking you out?'

Victoria shook her head with a wry half smile. 'I think I'm sort of past all that now, don't you?'

That caused Joanne to hoot with amusement. 'You're what—thirty-three? Trust me, there's plenty of time left for *all* of that.'

'But I already *had* that,' Victoria said. 'Even if Finn was interested—which, trust me, he isn't, he's totally focused on this project.' And getting petty revenge on his father. 'But, even if he was, I'm not. I was lucky enough to find true love and enjoy it for almost fourteen years. I'm not going to be bitter about losing it, but I'm not looking for a replacement either. Maybe one day, but not now.' And maybe never.

How could she look for love again, when that would be a betrayal of everything she'd had with Barnaby? How could she hunt down another fairy-tale ending, live *two* happy lives in one lifetime, when Harry didn't even get one?

'You know, life doesn't end with loss, Victoria.' Joanne's eyebrows had dipped in the middle into a serious frown. 'Look at me—I didn't even move here to Wishcliffe until after my husband died, and now I have a whole new career with the shop, a new social circle—'

'Yes, but you also moved here to get away

from people setting you up on blind dates,' Victoria reminded her.

Joanne threw up her hands in defeat—almost sending coffee flying over the stock behind her. 'Okay, okay. I take your point. Just...don't give up on happiness, okay? Even if that happiness doesn't look the same way you always thought it would.'

Victoria smiled. 'I won't, I promise. Even this—' she waved her coffee cup at the piles of paper '—has got me excited again. I didn't think I wanted to get involved, but it's nice to have the challenge.'

And when it was over, she could go back to the quiet, comfortable cocoon she'd built for herself, until she was ready to come out into whatever her new world looked like. When she was ready.

Eventually.

The phone rang again, and Victoria answered it absently.

'Wishcliffe Antiques—'

'I don't know where you live,' Finn interrupted her. 'I was all set to come up to Wishcliffe House, but you're not there any more, are you?'

Victoria thought of her tiny cottage by the beach, so far removed from her former home in style—if not actual distance—that it was almost laughable. And then she thought of Finn being there, in her safe space, her old world colliding with her new. Even Toby and Autumn hadn't been to the cottage except to drop off flowers and cake the day she'd moved in.

But this was work. And Finn's project *was* part of her new life, really.

She took a breath. 'Have you got a pen? I'll give you directions.'

# CHAPTER THREE

WISHCLIFFE VILLAGE WASN'T big, but somehow Victoria had managed to find a cottage that lay down roads Finn hadn't even known existed. He followed her directions—scribbled on a Post-it note stuck to his steering wheel—out of the main village and down country paths only just wide enough for his low-slung sports car to pass through, the bare branches of overhanging trees scraping the expensive paintwork as he drove, until eventually he saw something he recognised.

The sea.

Victoria's directions had taken him around the headland and to a tiny cove outside the village, and as he grew closer a small, squat white fisherman's cottage came into view. He parked just outside the gate, next to the hedgerow and the sea holly and grasses struggling to grow beside the white stone wall.

The cottage itself sat right on the edge of the beach, protected from the sea winds only by the curve of the cliffs and the stone wall around the property. Finn knocked on the bright blue door and, when there was no answer, wrapped his coat tighter around him and went to investigate.

It was only late afternoon, but already the sun was low over the sea, darkness beginning to encroach on the view. Still, as he reached the other side of the cottage he saw a figure down on the sand, her sunshine-yellow waterproof jacket a beacon in the twilight.

Victoria.

Finn picked his way through grasses and over rocks to the sand, and between the seaweed and shells that had washed up with the last tide, until he reached her.

'Kind of cold for a beach day, isn't it?' He dropped to sit on the sand beside her.

Victoria started at his voice, looking at him with surprise. 'What time is it? Sorry, I meant to head back in before you got here.'

'What were you doing out here?' Finn asked. 'Must have been pretty engrossing to lose all track of time.'

She glanced away. 'I was just…well, I was talking to the sea.'

And she was concerned about his state of mind? 'Did it talk back?'

That earned him an irritated look. 'It's not… When Harry was four or five, whenever he was scared or worried about something I used to tell him to give his worries to the sea. To talk it all out, and let the waves take it away.'

'I like that.' Finn stared out at the waves, white-tipped as they crashed up to the beach. 'I bet it worked too. Just saying things out loud makes them less scary sometimes, right?'

'That's the theory,' Victoria replied. 'Plus, if he did it when I was there, I got to find out what was worrying him too without him having to tell me direct.'

'Cunning.'

Victoria shrugged. 'Parent. Or, well. I was.'

It had been over a year, and she'd obviously trained herself to be able to talk about Harry and Barnaby without losing it, but still Finn could see the tension in the lines of her body, the way she hugged her knees a little closer to her chest.

'So what worries were you sharing with the sea?' he asked. 'Maybe I can help.'

'I wasn't, exactly. Well, I started to. But

in the end…' She sighed. 'I guess I was just talking to Barnaby. Again.'

'That makes sense,' Finn said, even though he wasn't totally sure it did.

'It's hard to imagine that he isn't still out there in the world somewhere,' Victoria admitted. 'So when I need to talk to him I come here, and make believe he can hear me.'

'Maybe he can,' Finn murmured. 'I used to do the same, after my mother died. I'd go out to her garden—even though it was all overgrown since she'd left—and talk to her. Until my father caught me one time and… well.' He shrugged.

He hadn't dared go back out to the little walled garden his mother had planted after the thrashing his father had given him for mentioning her name within the grounds of Clifford House. In fact, he hadn't even been back there since he'd moved in.

He wasn't sure he wanted to. Not yet.

'Can I ask what you were talking to Barnaby about today?' he asked.

Victoria shifted, stretching her legs out across the sand as she leant back on her hands. 'I was telling him about this project of yours. I suppose, every other time in my adult life that I've taken on something like this—a challenge—I'd talk it through with him first. Only this time, I had to decide for myself.'

'And you still want to do it?' Finn asked anxiously.

'I do,' Victoria replied. 'But I did have one question I wanted to ask, before we get started.'

'Anything.' He had all his answers prepared—why he was doing this, why it mattered to him, how much he was willing to spend, how far he would go.

But he wasn't ready for the bluntness of her question, all the same.

'Why did you stay away from Wishcliffe, after Barnaby and Harry died?'

'I didn't.' He blinked. 'I came to see you, remember? A month after the funerals.'

'To talk about Toby,' Victoria pointed out. 'You wanted to know how me staying at Wishcliffe another year would affect your business together.'

'That's not…not entirely true.' He never had been any good at lying to her, that was the problem. Even when he'd been sixteen, and he and Toby had got away with the most outrageous lies about their antics when old Viscount Wishcliffe had asked, once he was gone it had only ever taken one raised eye-brow from Victoria and he'd been spilling all the real details to her.

'Isn't it?'

'No! I mean, yes, I was worried about Toby—as my friend, not my business part-ner. But I was worried about you too.' She'd looked so small, so frail, and all he'd wanted to do was take her in his arms and keep her safe. But that wasn't his place. 'I wasn't avoid-ing you.'

An outright lie. Because that first visit after Barnaby's death, he'd known. Known that he couldn't take the guilt of looking at her and wanting her and knowing that she was Barnaby's—and Barnaby was gone.

When she'd been married, she was safe. He could look at her from afar and adore her, but never dream of doing anything about it. But that was just another thing that Barnaby's death had changed. Seeing her again, Finn hadn't fully trusted himself not to let on about how he felt, even accidentally. And he couldn't bear the idea of the horror in her eyes if she found out.

And so he'd stayed away.

'Yes, you were.' She sighed. 'It's fine. A lot of people did. I mean, after the first flurry of visits and cards and flowers, the sympathy sort of wore off, and then people didn't know what to say, I guess. I was just a sad young widow, and nobody likes to see that. It reminds them of the unfairness of the universe.'

'I remember that.' The memory came back suddenly, like a dream he'd half-forgotten on waking. 'When my mother left, and again when she died…it was the same. Well, sort of.' She'd been gone for over a year before her death, and his father hadn't allowed anyone to talk about her. But he remembered all his teachers, his friends, other family, worrying about him, making a big fuss over him for a week or two. And then it was as if the moment was over, and he was expected to be back to his normal self again.

As if he hadn't just lost his anchor in the world.

'I'm sorry,' he said. 'I should have visited, should have done more. I guess… I didn't think that there was anything I could do to help, and I was focused on Toby…'

'Of course you were. He's your best friend.' She shook her head. 'I shouldn't have said anything.'

'No.' He reached across and touched her cheek, turning it so she had to look at him.

'You're right. *You* are my friend too, and I should have been there for you, and I wasn't. I'm so sorry.'

Had she ever seen Finn look so serious? If she had, Victoria couldn't remember it. Maybe at the funerals, although she'd mostly blocked out all her memories of that day.

Swallowing, she looked away, and Finn's fingers fell from her face. 'You're here now.'

'Making you work for me.' Finn gave a hollow laugh. 'I don't think this counts as a sparkling example of friendship.'

'I don't know.'

Out at sea, the last of the daylight had disappeared, leaving only the pale moonlight shining on the water. She'd always thought the beach was magical at night. A place for secrets and mysteries.

She wasn't quite sure which Finn was yet.

'I think maybe I needed this project,' she admitted, her own secret to share. 'Joanne keeps telling me that there's still life after loss, but I think I'd been trying to avoid finding it. Hunting down antiques will get me out there, at least.'

'Toby said something similar,' Finn said mildly.

Victoria shot him a glare. 'I thought you said Toby didn't put you up to this?'

'He didn't,' Finn replied. 'But he was the one who insisted I didn't give up. He's the reason I called Joanne.'

'Humph. Well, I'm not thanking *him*.'

Finn laughed. 'You two really are just like brother and sister sometimes, aren't you?'

'He's the only family I've got left, really,' Victoria admitted. 'That's why I stayed so close to Wishcliffe. My mum died not long after I got married, remember? And my dad… well, he doesn't count. So the Blythes were my family. And now—'

'And now Toby's the only one left,' Finn finished for her. 'You know he feels the same, don't you?'

Victoria gave a stiff nod. 'I know. But he's got Autumn now, and the wedding to plan and, well. There's not much space for me. I need to find my own place.'

'Speaking of which, how about you show me this cottage of yours?' Finn got to his feet, brushing the sand from his jeans, then held a hand out to pull her up too. 'It looks a little smaller than your last place.'

Victoria laughed. 'Since my last place was

a twelve-bedroomed manor house, that's hardly surprising.'

'I don't know.' Finn shrugged. 'I figured you might have upgraded to a palace or something.'

They joked about her prospective housing options all the way back up the beach, past the little wind-battered gate with the peeling paint and in through the cheerful blue door that had sold the place to Victoria the first moment she'd seen it.

It was only once they were inside that Victoria realised how cold she'd got on the beach. January on the British coast wasn't ever the most hospitable weather, and she'd forgotten her gloves. But her thoughts had distracted her from the falling temperature.

'Do you want to light the fire?' She motioned towards the wood burning stove in the tiny lounge area. 'I think my hands are too numb.'

'Of course.'

As Finn set to work building the fire, Victoria stripped off her coat and scarf and opened the fridge to see what—if anything—she had to offer her guest. Not much, it turned out.

It wasn't that Victoria wasn't capable of cooking, it was just that, having had a live-in cook the whole time she'd lived at Wishcliffe House, she'd never really had much cause or opportunity. And since it was always just her at the cottage, she hadn't much felt like cooking cordon bleu meals for one. So all she had in were her staples. She hoped Finn wasn't expecting anything fancier.

'I can offer you hot chocolate and cheese on toast,' she said finally, as Finn returned to the kitchen counter. Behind him, she could see the wood burning stove blazing merrily.

'Sounds perfect,' he said.

'Sorry, I meant to go to the shops after work to get some real food, or at least a bottle of wine, but I guess I forgot.' Or, rather, she'd been preoccupied thinking about everything Joanne had said, and she'd wanted to get to the beach and talk it out with the waves.

'I said it was perfect,' Finn reminded her. 'I'm not much of a drinker anyway.'

He jumped up to perch on one of the kitchen stools at the breakfast bar that served in lieu of an actual dining table, and started rearranging the magnets on her fridge beside it. Used to Finn's inability not to fidget, Victoria rolled her eyes and set about preparing supper for them.

When she turned back, though, she was

surprised to find that her fridge poetry magnets didn't spell out any dirty limericks—presumably because Finn was too busy staring at the photo magnets she'd had printed when she'd moved in.

'I don't think I've ever seen this one before,' he said.

Victoria leaned across the bar to see which one he was looking at and laughed. 'I think that must have been taken the first summer I came to Wishcliffe.'

In the photo, Barnaby had his arms around her waist and they were leaning against one of the old apple trees in the Wishcliffe orchard. It would have been a beautiful, touching photo—if not for Toby and Finn hanging out of the nearby branches like monkeys, ready to pelt them with fruit.

'I remember.' Finn placed the magnet back on the fridge, his smile not quite reaching his eyes. 'That was a great summer.'

'It was.'

She wondered if he was remembering, like she was, how easy life had seemed back then. How the whole world seemed full of possibilities. As if they could do anything they wanted, and nothing could stop them, because they were together.

The sharp, piercing sound of the smoke alarm broke into her reverie and she spun, swearing, to rescue the burned cheese on toast from the grill, while Finn whipped a wet tea towel in the vague direction of the sensor.

'Sorry,' he said as the sound finally abated. 'I shouldn't have distracted you.'

Victoria tipped the toast in the bin and started again. 'Reminds me of trying to bake a birthday cake for Barnaby that time, when you and Toby insisted on helping, despite your obvious raging hangovers.'

'We helped!' Finn protested. 'Well, apart from that bit where Toby had to go and be sick. But I think the decorations really made it.'

'You spelt out "You're really old" with chocolate buttons on it while I was doing the washing-up.'

'Harsh but true,' Finn said with a solemn nod. 'The man needed to be told.'

Victoria rolled her eyes, then took the damp tea towel from him. 'Why don't you go wait in the lounge, and I'll bring this through when it's ready, okay?'

'Okay.' He hopped down and headed back towards the sofa. Victoria took a moment to watch him go, reconciling the man in front of her with the teenager of her memories.

Finn might have been gone from her life for a while but, now he was back, she was surprised how easy it was to fall into the old patterns of teasing and joking—as well as those few deeper, more meaningful moments in between.

She smiled to herself as she set about grating more cheese.

If nothing else, it seemed like this revenge project of his might at least have brought her friend back to her. And she couldn't be sorry about that.


Considering he was only really used to spending time with her in the vast spaces of Wishcliffe House, Finn was surprised how well the cosy cottage by the sea suited Victoria. It was tiny—he couldn't imagine there was more than one bedroom—but he could see instantly why she'd chosen it. It felt cocooning, safe, in a way he imagined she hadn't much lately.

And she could step outside and talk to Barnaby, Harry and the waves whenever she wanted.

Loitering in the lounge, he picked up another photo—this one a proper framed print. A family portrait—Victoria, Barnaby and Harry all together on the beach, grinning at each other with smiles that screamed of love and contentment.

Finn had never really thought much about True Love outside of fairy tales and movies, until the summer Barnaby had brought Victoria home to Wishcliffe. Anyone who'd seen them together couldn't help but know that they were in the presence of the real thing. He'd never doubted, after that, the idea that true love was real.

But he also knew it was rare. Precious. And not for everybody. Not for him, chances were, or he'd have found it already.

His parents certainly hadn't found it, or many of the people he'd met out on the road, building the business. Seemed to him that almost everybody was either unhappy in their marriage, cheating on their spouse, divorcing—or all three.

Toby and Autumn, Finn suspected, might be another exception, despite their inauspicious start. Even the first morning he'd found them together he'd seen the spark of it. And that only seemed to have grown over the winter.

Now they were planning their second wedding—since none of their friends or family had got to attend their first impulsive Vegas one—and soon, Finn was sure, they'd be a family of three or four, or more. Settling down as the next generation at Wishcliffe House.

While Victoria hid down here in her cosy cottage.

He'd wondered over the years why Victoria and Barnaby had never had more children. But then he'd seen her red eyes and haunted face on a visit and Toby had obliquely warned him that it wasn't a topic for discussion, and they'd taken Harry out to kick a ball about for a while instead.

Later, he'd learned about the miscarriages—from Victoria herself in the end, one quiet summer evening when they'd been talking on the terrace. How there'd been two before they had Harry, and another two since. How the doctors thought it was best not to try any longer.

More losses she'd had to bear, but at least she'd had Barnaby at her side for those, and Harry in her arms.

Now it was just her.

'Cheese on toast.' Victoria placed a large plate in the centre of the small coffee table.

Finn's mouth started salivating at the scent. 'Did you make it the way you always used to? With the…whatever it was under the cheese?'

'Mango chutney,' Victoria said. 'And yes. Now, come grab your hot chocolate.'

They settled down together on the one small sofa, opposite the fire, and tucked into the cheese on toast—which was every bit as good as Finn remembered from drunken evenings at Wishcliffe, after he and Toby had staggered home from the pub and persuaded Victoria to make it for them.

While they ate, she filled him in on the progress she'd made, organising their task ahead.

'Once we've finished eating, I need you to look through the files,' she said around a mouthful of toast crumbs. 'Let me know if you agree with how I categorised everything.'

He cleared the plates and cups away, washing them up in the single sink under the window, while she spread out the photos and papers he'd given her on the coffee table. When he'd handed the files over, they'd been a mishmash of everything he'd been able to collect about Clifford House—bills of sale for various antiques, photos and press clippings from events held there, magazine spreads filled with descriptions of the house, accompanied with photos of his parents sitting stiffly beside each other, insurance documents detailing the contents of various rooms.

Now, every piece of paper had a coloured flag attached, and Finn could see Victoria's precise sloping writing on each note.

'This pile here is pieces that seemed like the cornerstone ones—the antiques we should try to track down and buy back if possible,' Victoria explained. That pile, Finn noticed, was significantly smaller than the other two. 'The second pile is items I think we can probably buy similar antiques to—same period or general feel, at least.'

'And the third pile?' The largest one, of course.

Victoria sighed. 'Those are the ones where you might want to consider looking for something different. Either they're going to be impossible to match, or they're not worth the money you'd have to pay to get them. They won't add much to the aesthetic, and I don't think they're a good place to focus our energy.'

Finn nodded slowly. 'That makes sense, I

suppose.' Even if something inside him ran-kled at letting any of his heritage go with-out a fight. 'So you want me to check there's nothing in piles two or three that needs to be in the first pile.'

'Or vice versa,' she replied, although she didn't sound too optimistic about that likeli-hood.

She'd done a great job, Finn thought, as he started going through the papers. From the mess he'd given her, she'd developed de-tailed lists with notes on provenance and es-timated costs—one or two of which did make him wince, after all—and whittled down the whole thing until it felt almost achievable.

There was only one item he pulled out of the second pile and added back to the first.

'Really?' Victoria asked as she stared at the photo of a mantel clock that was probably less than two hundred years old. 'Why that? As far as I could tell, it didn't have any dis-tinctive features to link it to Clifford House.' Most of the items in the first pile, Finn had noticed, were items with an obvious and marked connection to the house itself—like the china platter and matching soup tureen with the painting of the house's facade in blue on the white porcelain.

'My great-grandfather was given that clock by some minor royal or another,' he said. 'Granddad used to go on and on about it. My father would definitely notice if we didn't get that one back.'

Victoria placed the photo of the clock onto the first pile. 'I can't believe your father wouldn't have kept at least *some* of these things when he moved out of Clifford House. Is it possible I'm going to end up trying to buy them back from him?'

Finn shook his head. 'Not a chance.' When her brow furrowed in confusion, he explained. 'If he still owned them, they'd come to me when he died. He can't risk that.'

'Couldn't he just change his will?' Victoria asked.

'Apparently not. One of my cannier ancestors legally tied the Lord's possessions to the title, so they have to be passed down to me along with that. When I become Lord Clifford, I get everything that my father owns. Which is why, of course, he's sold as much of it as he possibly can and is now working his way through the proceeds in the bars and casinos of the world. To keep it all out of my hands.' Victoria looked like she might ask him to talk about his feelings for his father any second, which Finn had no desire to do, so he changed the subject quickly. 'Anyway, now you've got all this lot sorted, what's our first move? Go after the items in pile one?'

'Actually, no.' From her expression, Finn suspected he hadn't got away with avoiding that conversation for ever, but for now she was letting him off the hook. 'Those are going to take some time—I need to track down who your father sold them to, whether they've been sold on since, and then start negotiations to see if we can get them back. I'll be working on all of that, of course. But in the meantime I'm taking you to one of my favourite places in the world to make a start on piles two and three.'

'Oh? Where's that?' As if he wouldn't go anywhere she wanted when the excitement in her voice at the idea was so palpable.

'Portobello Road Market, London.'

# CHAPTER FOUR

THE FOLLOWING SATURDAY morning Victoria caught an early train up to London, coffee and croissant from the stand at the station in her hand, and tried not to think about how this was the first time she'd visited the city since Barnaby and Harry died.

It hadn't been intentional, the way her world had shrunk to Wishcliffe House and the village over the last year and a bit. There'd just been so much to do, especially while Toby was still away. It had been easier to stay close to home—even if it meant living with the memories every day.

By the time she'd been ready to move out to her little cottage on the edge of the village, she'd not left Wishcliffe in a year. And unpacking her new home, starting her new job, it had all kept her busy enough that she hadn't even really noticed how tied to Wish-cliffe she'd become.

A day in London would do her good—especially a day pottering around Portobello Road. And a day with Finn…well, that would probably do their friendship some good too. Spending the evening with him at her cottage had reminded her how much she enjoyed his company—his dry wit, his way of seeing past the words she was actually saying but not pressing deeper when she obviously didn't want to talk about something.

He'd been almost as close to Barnaby as Toby had. He had been Harry's godfather, for heaven's sake. He knew exactly what she'd lost and he felt that pain too, in his own way.

With him, she didn't have to pretend that everything was okay now, and that made her feel more relaxed than she'd have imagined it could.

While the train snaked its way through the English countryside and into the city, Victoria studied the list she'd made, with Finn's help, to guide their search that day. By the time her carriage halted at the platform at Victoria Station, she had a good feel for her priorities—and she was itching to get started.

She took the Circle Line clockwise to Notting Hill Gate, where she found Finn waiting for her, as arranged. He, Victoria noted, did not look like he'd been up since stupid o'clock that morning to get there before all the good stuff was sold. Instead, he looked well-rested and relaxed in his jeans and a cream wool jumper over a navy shirt.

She'd feel resentful, but he handed her a cup of coffee and she decided to forgive him after the first sip, as rich, earthy notes overtook her senses.

'This tastes amazing.' She checked the cup for a logo, but it was blank. 'Where did you get it?'

'There's a little pop-up stand by my flat, only there on a Saturday,' he explained. 'I always get a coffee there to start my weekend if I'm in town. I've never tasted coffee like it anywhere else.'

'I forgot how close your flat is to Notting Hill,' Victoria admitted. 'This is hardly a special day out for you. You must come here all the time.'

'Actually, I haven't been in years.' Finn motioned towards the street and they started walking in the direction of the market. 'I guess it's that thing where, when you can visit something any time you like, you never have the urgency to make you actually go.'

'I suppose.' But Victoria knew that if she lived near the famous Portobello Road Market, nothing would tear her away every Saturday.

The start of the market was only a short walk from the Tube. Victoria finished her coffee just as the first stalls came into view, and she popped the cup into the nearest recycling bin before fishing her list out of her bag as they reached the market itself.

'There's a plan, I take it?' Finn eyed the list, and she smiled to see the slight apprehension in his gaze.

Some women liked shoe shopping. Some could shop for clothes for days. Or books, or power tools, or make-up.

Victoria had no interest in most of those. But when it came to shopping for antiques, she had real dedication. She had to, to get the best pieces. And that was why Finn had hired her, wasn't it?

'Of course there's a plan.' There were hundreds of stalls lining Portobello Road on a Saturday morning, not to mention all the permanent shops and the antique arcades snaking off the Main Street. Going in without a plan would be foolish.

'So, where do we start?' Finn asked.

Victoria stood for a moment, letting the vibrancy of the market sweep over her. The bright colours of the cloths on the market stall tables, laden with glinting treasures that just waited to be discovered. The vintage signs hanging from higher bars, their faded paints still bright against the grey of the January sky. Silver tea services hung from hooks on rails above the stalls, the flags and signs of the shops and arcades high on the buildings, and the clash of colours of vintage clothing hanging on rails.

And then there were the sounds and the scents. The rising chatter and calls of the shoppers and the sellers, frozen breaths puffing out with every offer, every sale. The scent of brass polish, musty books, mingled with fresh coffee and cooking meat from the food stalls further down.

*I just wish I could have brought Harry to see this.*

He'd always been too young, or uninterested, or there'd been too much else to do on the estate. Somehow, it had just never been the right time—and now there was no time left.

She let the loss settle for a moment, the way she'd learned to deal with all these reminders, then let it float away again. Acknowledged, examined—but not letting it take over her day. That was the only way she'd found that helped her deal with the waves of grief that still hit her most days.

But she was here, at the world-famous Portobello Road, one of her favourite places in the world. And she wasn't going to waste the day thinking of what might have been.

She put her list back in her bag.

'You know what? Let's just get a feel for the place first, yeah?'

Finn's face brightened at her words. 'Sounds good to me! And maybe grab another coffee and a bite to eat?'

'Definitely that,' Victoria said with a laugh.

'Well, then.' Finn held out an arm to her, and she slipped her hand into the crook of his elbow as if it were the most natural thing in the world. 'Let's shop.'

He felt like he was watching Victoria come to life again.

After all the tragedy and pain of the last

year, and all the struggle and hard work at Wishcliffe even before that, as Finn followed Victoria from stall to stall along Portobello Road it was as if he were seeing her step back in time. Not because of the age of the objects she was studying, but because she seemed to give up her cares and worries with every step. Her shoulders lowered, her walk became freer, her arms swinging carelessly at her sides.

And she *smiled*.

Not the careful, contained smile he'd seen since they'd reconnected over his antiques project. And definitely not the sad, unsteady smile he'd seen right after the accident. Not even the stressed but happy smile he'd seen so often before that, when the dark circles had almost overshadowed her sparkling eyes.

This smile was the one he'd fallen for when he was sixteen. The one that lit up the air around her with sheer infectious joy.

He wasn't the only one who'd noticed it either. The traders and shoppers at Portobello Road Market might not know what it meant to Finn to see that smile again, but they were affected by it all the same. They smiled back, despite themselves. They offered discounts Finn was almost certain they wouldn't have offered to most. The pimply teenager who served them their coffees and containers of curry and rice even threw in extra onion bhajis without being asked.

Victoria's smile infected the whole market, and it lightened Finn's heart to see it.

'So, where next?' Finn wiped mango chutney from his fingers and took her carton from her to dispose of. 'Is it time to look at the list again?'

Victoria nodded and, taking the piece of paper from her bag, unfolded it and smoothed it out over her knee. 'I got a good idea of what sort of things we can cross off here today just wandering around.'

'Not to mention the hand mirror and the brush set you convinced that poor bloke on the silver stall to put aside for you for later,' Finn added. He'd definitely got the feeling the man wouldn't have done it for anybody but Victoria.

'Yes—we mustn't forget to go back and pick those up.' Victoria frowned down at her list. 'Actually, there was one particular shop I wanted to show you that we haven't visited yet. I think we might have a good chance of replacing some of the family china there.' She looked up with a hopeful smile that made him wonder if there was something special about this shop. A reason she'd saved it until now.

'Then let's go,' he said.

He let Victoria lead the way, as he had all day. He'd half expected her to make a beeline for one of the brightly coloured shops on the main street, but instead she weaved through the crowd and the stalls for a nondescript entrance crammed between two larger shops. There was no sign above the arched entryway, and no indication that there were any antiques for sale there at all.

Frowning, Finn followed as Victoria confidently picked her way down the narrow alleyway, stepping over wicker baskets and dodging tattered pennants hanging overhead.

'Georgie?' she called out, and he saw that she'd stepped out of the alleyway into—

Into a wonderland.

Whether the shop existed outside of the usual dimensions of space and time or was somehow tucked away along the back of the other shops on Portobello Road, Finn wasn't entirely sure—although he hoped it was the latter. Either way, it ran only a few metres deep but what seemed like half a mile long. Every inch of the space was taken up with towering shelves, displays, chairs and tables—all save the narrow walkways between them. And it wasn't only the ground that was filled; overhead hung racks heavy with gleaming pots and pans, vintage model aircraft paused in flight between the antiques and shelves stacked with books and knick-knacks all the way to the rafters.

It was as if the entirety of the street outside had been crammed inside the confines of one dark and narrow shop.

'Victoria Capon—no, Victoria Blythe now, isn't it? I never remember that.' A tall, grey-haired man in glasses eased his slender frame between two bookcases and emerged into the small entrance area where they stood. 'As I live and breathe, it is you! To what do I owe this pleasure, Your Ladyship?' He sketched a small bow then caught the porcelain pig he knocked off the nearest sideboard without missing a beat.

'Hello, Georgie.' She reached over to hug the older man, moving carefully to avoid dislodging any other treasures, Finn noticed. 'I'm sorry it's been a while. Things have been—'

'I heard.' Georgie's long face was solemn. 'I was so very sorry, my dear.'

Victoria's smile wavered, and Finn reached out to squeeze her hand.

'But you're here on a mission today, I can tell!' Georgie swept her up with an arm around her shoulder, his movements almost birdlike in their jerkiness as he nudged her deeper into the labyrinth of his shop. Finn followed behind, feeling more out of place than he'd felt anywhere since he'd left Clifford House at eighteen.

'I'm helping my friend refurnish his family home,' Victoria explained. 'Here's some of the items we're looking for…'

Georgie snatched the list from her hand as soon as it was out of her bag, his lips moving along with his eyes as he scanned through it, mumbling to himself.

'Hmm, I see, and yes—ah!—of course.' He looked up, eyes bright. 'You'll want the china department, then?'

He spun on his heel and set out into the maze of shelves.

'Are there actual *departments* to this place?' Finn kept his voice low as they followed. 'I thought every new delivery was just dumped on top of the last.'

'That's because you're not looking closely enough, young man!' Georgie's voice floated back around shelves and boxes, and Finn gave Victoria an incredulous look.

She shrugged. 'Georgie knows where every single item of his stock is at all times. And his hearing is *excellent*.'

Finn decided to keep the rest of his observations to himself, until they were back outside.

True to his word, Georgie took them straight to an aisle filled with china—some on display on Welsh dressers, others stacked up on shelves and in boxes.

'You should find something to suit your purposes here,' he said, waving a hand expressively and narrowly missing a willow pattern teapot that sat precariously close to the edge of a shelf. 'I suggest you try the dresser at the end—the turquoise one. Now, if you'll excuse me, I believe I have another customer.'

He disappeared off into the stacks at least a few seconds before the bell on the front desk rang. 'How did he know?' Finn wondered aloud.

'Excellent hearing, my boy!' Georgie's voice floated back.

Finn shook his head, decided to chalk it all up to some sort of Harry Potter nonsense, and moved on.

He found Victoria already crouched down beside the turquoise dresser, her head inside the giant piece of furniture. 'Found what you're looking for in there?'

'Almost,' her voice came back, muffled. 'Hang on…'

Finally she emerged triumphant, holding up a large dinner plate with a hunting scene painted on it. 'Does this look like the Clifford family china?'

Finn studied it. Unnecessary cruelty, aristocratic pursuits and a sense of self-importance? Check. 'Almost exactly.'

'It's the same artist.' Victoria handed the plate to him to hold, then dived back inside. 'Slightly different imagery, but the same feel. I think it should pass muster.' She pulled out a stack of side plates, looked at the pictures and shuddered.

'I guess the family china at Wishcliffe is rather less bloodthirsty?' He had to admit, despite the many meals he'd eaten at that dining table, he wasn't sure he could describe the plates if his life depended on it.

'Just a bit.' Victoria reached up and pulled another plate from the shelf of the next dresser along. 'It's more like this—farming labourers and harvest-themed.'

What was wrong with plain white china, that was what Finn would like to know. Or, at a push, recyclable paper plates. Most of the time he ended up eating takeaway from a carton, anyway.

'Do you miss it?' he asked as she replaced the china.

'The Wishcliffe dinner plates?' Victoria frowned. 'Not particularly.'

'I meant all of it. You know, the grandeur of Wishcliffe, all the family heirlooms, passed down through the generations, that sort of thing.' Her cottage, while lovely, was rather a step down from what she'd been used to, the last ten years or so.

Victoria considered his question properly this time, if the contemplative look on her face was anything to go by. 'Not really. I mean, there are spots around the house that I miss—the orchard, for instance, or my little study on the top floor. The way the sun came into the library in the late afternoon, that sort of thing. But the actual antiques? To be honest, most of them weren't really my style.'

Finn gazed pointedly around the Aladdin's cave of treasures she'd brought him to, while remembering every adoring look she'd given an antique on their stroll through the market.

'Oh, I love antiques,' she clarified. 'I just meant that if I was furnishing a place from scratch, those wouldn't be the pieces *I'd* choose. Not because they're not beautiful, but because half the fun is finding the pieces that really speak to you.' She shrugged. 'Barnaby always loved them, though, because they were part of his family. That makes a difference too, I think.'

Finn thought about her tiny cottage with its sparse furnishings, and wondered if she was still trying to find those pieces that were hers, now she was out in the world alone. 'Is there anything here that speaks to you?'

Victoria grinned. 'Oh, masses. Like…' She reached behind her to yet another sideboard and pulled up a cream coffee cup with tiny green stars on it, and a matching saucer in the same green. As she tilted the cup, he saw the inside was green too. 'These. They're from the nineteen-fifties or early sixties, by Susie Cooper. Georgie doesn't have a whole set here, I don't think. But there's a few different colours for the saucers and cups, all with the same green star design.'

'Of course you picked a coffee cup,' Finn said. The woman was a fiend for her caffeine. 'They're pretty.'

She studied the cup again before replacing it on the sideboard. 'I like them. But they never fitted with the aesthetic at Wishcliffe and, besides, it wasn't like we didn't have enough china as it was. Come on. We need to go pay for this lot and ask Georgie to pack and ship it to Clifford House. Because there's no way I'm carrying it on the train.'

It was already dark by the time she made it back to Victoria Station that evening. Finn had insisted on seeing her to her train, even though she'd pointed out that she wasn't exactly carrying priceless antiques with her— they'd arranged for all their purchases either to be sent on or taken them back to Finn's London flat in a taxi to be couriered later. Still, she was glad of the company when it emerged that her train was delayed for an hour, and they'd had time to grab a quick dinner at a restaurant around the corner.

Finally, though, it was time to head back to Wishcliffe.

'I had a nice day today,' Finn said as they walked towards her platform. 'Turns out this revenge malarky is a lot more fun than I'd thought it would be.'

She couldn't help but laugh at that. 'Well, as long as it's not boring you already.'

'I could never be bored, hanging out with you.'

Probably he was just saying it to make her feel good, but it sent a warm rush through her all the same.

'I had a great day too,' she admitted. 'I wasn't sure about this revenge plot of yours but... I think I'm coming round.'

'Now you know that it means spending someone else's money on antiques you can't afford?'

'Basically, yeah.' Victoria checked her ticket again. 'This is my carriage. I guess I'll see you in a few weeks? For Derbyshire?' Over dinner they'd plotted out their next moves, including a trip to one of her favourite antique emporiums in the Peak District. If Finn had thought that Georgie's was stuffed with antiques, The Mill was going to blow him away.

Finn nodded. 'I'll check it out and book us somewhere to stay for the night.'

'That would be great, thanks.' She stepped up onto the train, pausing when he reached out and grabbed her arm.

'Hang on. I just...' He reached into the

leather satchel he carried and pulled out something wrapped in tissue paper. 'For you. Well, for your coffee. The amount of it you drink, you deserve a decent cup.'

Victoria tore back just enough of the carefully wrapped paper to see the green stars of the Susie Cooper cup and saucer she'd admired winking back at her.

'You bought it for me? Why? And, more to the point, when?' They'd been together all day. When could he have doubled back to get it?

Finn chuckled. 'I had an ally. Remember when Georgie sent you off to try and find that missing dinner plate, only to discover it under the desk after all?'

Of course. Georgie was an old softie at heart. 'Well, thank you. I love it. But you shouldn't have.'

'Yes, I should,' Finn replied. 'Think of it as a very small thank you for everything you're doing.'

'Hmm. Maybe I should get Joanne to put up my fee then…' She tapped a finger against her jaw as if really considering it, and Finn barked a laugh. 'Really, thank you.'

'You're welcome.' Down the platform, the conductor blew his whistle. 'Time to go.'

She tucked her treasure safely in her bag, then reached out of the train door to hug Finn goodbye.

'See you soon.' And as she'd done a hundred times since she'd met him, she placed a quick kiss on his cheek as he did the same for her.

But maybe the height of the train made a difference, or the other passengers made the carriage shift. Because she missed.

Not completely. Just enough for her mouth to graze the edge of his, before they both pulled back.

Just close enough to send a surge of something long forgotten racing through her. A heat, an excitement, a possibility that she'd thought only existed in the past for her.

An attraction.

She stumbled back, hoping she wasn't blushing, and waved through the glass as the doors closed and the train jerked into motion. Gazed backwards as Finn stood stock-still on the platform, watching her go.

Then she went to find her seat and resolutely did not think about what that flash of feeling could mean.

She just hoped Finn would have forgotten the awkward moment by the time they travelled to Derbyshire together next month.

# CHAPTER FIVE

'YOU'VE BEEN SUMMONED for dinner too then, I take it?' Finn said when his knock on the front door of Wishcliffe House was answered by Victoria rather than Toby or Autumn.

'I have.' She stepped back to let him inside. 'Although they didn't tell me you were coming.'

'Last minute addition. I told them I'd be at Clifford House tonight, since we're heading up to Derbyshire tomorrow anyway, so they invited me for dinner.' Finn shucked off his heavy winter coat and hung it over a leather wingback chair in front of the roaring fire that filled the fireplace in the centre of the entrance hall. 'Where are the Viscount and his lady, anyway?'

It was still weird to think of Toby as Viscount Wishcliffe when for so long it had been his father, and then Barnaby. Toby was never supposed to inherit, but now he'd settled into the role it seemed to suit him.

'In the study, I think. Ah—I wouldn't go in there if I were you,' Victoria added as he moved towards the corridor that led to the Viscount's study. Her amused tone indicated exactly what he was likely to discover if he opened the door and, really, Finn had seen enough of his best friend's bare behind in the showers after PE at school to ever need to see it again as an adult.

Finn paused, raising his eyebrows. 'Really? When they have *guests*?'

'I don't think we count as guests,' Victoria replied. 'We're family.'

The warmth he felt at being considered family easily outweighed the minor annoyance of Toby and Autumn being too *busy* to meet them—and even balanced out the frustration that his best friend was now in the kind of blissful relationship that resulted in regular, just-can't-wait-to-have-you sex in inappropriate places.

Finn had never really wanted or hoped for that kind of relationship—and certainly not marriage. From what he'd seen, the men in his family weren't genetically predisposed to success in love or matrimony, and from what he knew of himself, he couldn't imagine that *he'd* be the one to break that curse.

His parents' marriage had made everyone around them miserable, themselves most of all, until his mother had walked out and left young Finn with a man who despised him, for the love of a Spaniard who got her killed by driving too fast on the coastal roads over in his home country. From what little he remembered, his grandparents' marriage had only been more successful in the sense that they'd stayed married and living, nominally, in the same house. His grandfather had spent most of his time in London, and Finn was almost certain he'd never actually seen the two of them in the same room at the same time.

No, he'd come to terms with the idea of remaining a sole agent a long time ago. If nothing else, it wouldn't be fair to drag anyone else into the seething resentment and betrayal that was his family life. While he was focused on gaining his revenge on his father, there wasn't any space for any softer feelings, really.

Mostly, his need for human touch and affection could be fulfilled by short-lived romances with women who knew exactly what he was—and wasn't—offering and didn't want any more from him anyway.

But he still missed…something sometimes. Companionship, perhaps. Having someone to laugh with, share secrets with. For so long he'd been focused on building the business, making enough money to put his plans into action. And since his revenge project had really taken off, starting nine months ago with the long and tedious negotiations that had allowed him to buy back Clifford House, he hadn't even had time or focus for finding one of those short-term romances he was so good at.

Maybe he was just missing sex. The fact that Toby had managed to get married, fall in love and live happily ever after in the time since Finn last had another person in his bed at night was horrifying—and unexpected. If asked to place bets on which of the two of them was more likely to have a one-night stand in Vegas, Finn knew he'd be the odds-on favourite.

Instead, he'd been back in his hotel room running numbers with his accountant via a video call. And the closest he'd got to a woman recently was the soft press of Victoria's lips against the corner of his mouth at the station, before the train had whisked her away. He knew that she'd meant nothing at all by it—in fact, from the way she'd blushed after, he imagined she was horrified at missing his cheek. But that hadn't stopped him replaying the moment over and over in his mind during the two weeks since. Imagining what might have happened next if she *had* meant it. If he'd tugged her off that train and into his arms and—

Victoria was watching him, he realised belatedly, looking as though she were trying to read his mind. He'd never been so thankful that telepathy didn't exist.

Forcing a smile, Finn threw himself into the nearest chair and motioned for Victoria to take the seat opposite him. Time to get his thoughts back on the things that mattered— buying back everything his father had sold and rubbing his nose in it.

'Since we've got some time, apparently, why don't you fill me in on where we are with the family heirlooms you've been tracing?'

Victoria's face lit up as she pulled her ever-present file out of her bag and flipped through it to find the right section. 'Actually, things are going really well!'

Finn sat back and let her words wash over

him, as she talked about the dealers she'd spoken to, the leads she'd followed and the progress she'd made. The excitement on her face, the way she spoke with her hands, her words coming together faster and faster as she reached her biggest triumphs—they all confirmed what Finn already knew.

Firstly, that he'd been right to bring her on board—not just for her obvious expertise and successes, but because she needed it as much as he needed her.

And secondly, that no woman in the world was as beautiful as Victoria Blythe talking about something that mattered to her.

Eventually, though, Toby and Autumn emerged from the study—looking more than a little ruffled—and it was time for dinner. The four of them took their seats at one end of the giant dining table and chatted like old friends through starters and mains and a bottle of wine.

It was only once they reached the desserts that Finn spotted the slight undercurrent between the newlyweds. A hum of excited apprehension, he decided, as he honed in on it. The feeling that there was something more to come than an apple crumble with cream.

And then he realised that while four glasses

of wine had been poured, only three were now empty.

Toby and Autumn exchanged another secret glance, and Finn knew exactly what was coming next. Which was why he was already watching Victoria when Toby spoke.

'Actually, we did have another reason for asking the two of you to join us tonight. We've got some news. We're, uh, expecting a baby!'

The night air was cool and fresh in the apple orchard, the February wind tempered by the trees around her. Victoria sucked in deep breaths and tried to calm her hammering heart as she leant against the low stone wall that surrounded the orchard.

She thought she'd done okay. She'd realised, seconds before Toby had spoken, exactly what he was going to say, and she'd schooled her expression into one of untempered joy and happiness. Which *was* what she felt for her friends, so it wasn't that hard.

It just wasn't what she felt for herself.

Still, this was their big exciting news and she wasn't going to be the one to ruin it by making the moment all about her. So she'd smiled and congratulated them and hugged them both. She'd peppered Autumn with questions about how she was feeling and when her due date was and her upcoming twelve-week scan, all through dessert. She'd grinned and told them she was looking forward to being Auntie Victoria and spoiling their child rotten, laughing when Finn had decided they should team up and get the kid hyped up on sugar and excitement before going home for the night and leaving Toby and Autumn to deal with the consequences.

'Just like we used to do with Harry,' Toby had laughed, and Victoria's heart had almost broken.

But she'd kept smiling. She'd moved them all past the awkward moment with talk about embarrassing family names they might choose and which room they were planning to use for the nursery and if they wanted to redecorate.

She'd kept talking and talking and smiling and smiling until the coffees were finished and she'd been able to excuse herself for a moment.

Then she'd run to the orchard for some fresh air and the space to just *feel*.

'Are you okay?' Finn's voice cut through the dark air around her, warm and concerned.

'I'm fine,' she lied. 'Just needed some air after all that wine.' She'd drunk barely more than a glass, but hopefully Finn wouldn't have noticed that.

'Right.' Yeah, he'd noticed. Seemed like Finn noticed everything.

He leaned against the wall beside her, close enough that she could feel the warmth of him through their clothes.

'I'm not saying… I mean, I get it if you don't want to talk to me about it,' he said after a moment. 'But honestly? Of course you're not going to be okay after that news. So, if you *do* want to talk, well. I'm here.'

Victoria looked down at the damp grass at her feet, black in the moonlight, to hide her smile. Finn wasn't exactly the obvious choice for a heart-to-heart, but she was surprised to find she felt more comfortable with him beside her than she had alone.

'I am genuinely happy for them,' she said.

'Of course you are. It's great news and you're a nice person.' Finn tilted his head to look at her, and she couldn't help but meet his understanding gaze. 'That doesn't mean you can't *also* feel sad, or mad, or lost, or whatever else you're feeling right now. People can feel more than one thing at once. Or so I've heard.'

Victoria let out a sigh. 'I think I have too many feelings to articulate them all. Or even keep them straight in my head.' Yes, she was happy for her friends. But that didn't stop the terrible yawning gulf of loss inside her at the idea that another baby would grow up at Wishcliffe in Harry's place. Or the fury that raged in her heart that he'd had that life taken from him. Or the pain because she was still there to see it all, without her husband and son.

Finn slipped his hand into hers and squeezed. Without thinking, Victoria let her head rest against his shoulder, feeling his warmth and his concern flowing through her where they were joined.

'The way I see it, you're allowed as many feelings as you need,' he said softly. 'And you can have them all at the same time, even if they seem totally contradictory.'

'I guess so.'

'And I'd imagine Toby is feeling some of them right now too. Because, as happy as he is with Autumn and a baby on the way…you know he hasn't forgotten about Barnaby and

Harry.' He paused. 'And neither have I. We never will.'

'So what do we do?' she asked, hoping he'd have the answers that were still evading her. 'When our feelings are at such opposite ends of the spectrum that it feels like they're tearing us apart?'

A longer pause this time. Finn huffed a breath against the top of her head, resting his lips against her hair in an almost kiss.

'I guess we just keep feeling them. And we trust each other to help keep us together.'

*Trust each other.*

Suddenly, one of those other feelings that was swirling around inside her tonight started to make sense. A feeling that she wasn't alone any more. For the whole first year after the accident, while Toby was away tying up his business loose ends and Finn was off keeping his best friend on an even keel, she'd felt alone. Not just lonely, but utterly alone in her loss. In her feelings.

Even at Wishcliffe House, surrounded by all the people who made their living from the estate—friends, colleagues, everybody— she'd still felt alone. Because none of them understood.

But now Toby and Finn were back. Toby

had lost a brother, a nephew. And Finn had lost the family he'd chosen over his own, years before. It wasn't the same, but it didn't need to be. The grief was still there, deep and empty, and she wasn't alone in it.

That whole year, she'd been afraid that if she let the grief out, it would swallow her whole.

Oh, she'd done all the exercises her therapist recommended, practised feeling the emotions and letting them pass, journalled her moods and everything else. But none of it had been more than a mask for that huge hole at her centre.

But now she had company in it, that hole didn't feel quite so vast, or so empty.

'Thank you,' she murmured.

'For what?' Finn asked, his words warm against her hair.

'For finding me.' She didn't add that she didn't just mean tonight. She meant all of it—the project, London, taking her out of herself and into the world again.

She suspected Finn knew, all the same.

'We should get back inside.' She pulled away, just enough to look up at him. 'I'm feeling better, I promise.'

Finn nodded, but she could still see the

concern in his eyes. The same concern she'd felt even before Toby had made his announcement. She'd almost forgotten, in the tumult of her emotions after. But Finn had been watching her in that moment. Worrying about her.

Victoria wasn't sure what she'd done to deserve a friend like Finn Clifford, but she was damn glad to have him.

Then he smiled, warm and wide, and pressed a kiss to her forehead. A brotherly kiss. A friendly kiss. Not even as close to a real kiss as her miss on the train platform had been.

The heat surged through her at his touch, all the same. And Victoria realised, almost too late, that there were some other feelings she hadn't dealt with or even acknowledged yet.

Lust. Want. For Finn, a man she'd known since he was a gangly teenager and had never considered as anything but a friend.

And with it came the counterpoint emotions of guilt and betrayal, rising up in her throat like acid. Because how could she feel that when the love of her life was dead?

Unaware of her inner turmoil, Finn had already turned back towards the house. 'Come on. We've got an early start tomorrow if we want to make Derbyshire in time for some serious antique hunting.'

Well, if four hours trapped in a car together didn't help her make sense of her feelings, Victoria couldn't imagine what would.

They set out early the next morning, February mist curling around the trees and gateposts as they left Wishcliffe village and headed north. Victoria was quiet, clutching her travel coffee mug close and staring out of the window as Finn pulled the car onto the main road. He left her to her thoughts, assuming that last night's news was still occupying her.

For himself, it wasn't Toby and Autumn's happy news that kept his brain busy. Instead, it was the way that Victoria had looked up at him, something behind her eyes that he wasn't used to seeing. Those warring emotions she'd spoken of seemed almost visible in her conflicted gaze—only he had the strangest feeling she hadn't been thinking of the new baby, but him. It was the same look he'd seen behind the blushes as her train had pulled away from the platform in London.

What was it that was causing her to fight with herself so?

He hoped he'd find out over the next day

or two together. But for the time being he put on the radio and let her think—only turning it down a little as they passed London and she fell asleep, her cheek resting on her coat, against the window.

They made good time, stopping only to refuel—the car and themselves—and pick up more coffees, and arrived in the pretty village of Castleton, where he'd booked their room for the night, just after lunch.

'Are you hungry?' Finn asked, eyeing the local pub they'd be staying at. It looked busy enough, bustling with a few tourists despite the February gloom, and a sign in the window said *No Vacancies*, always a good indication of a popular place to stay. The website had looked nice, but it was always hard to tell until he saw a place in person. He hoped Victoria would like it.

But Victoria shook her head. 'That full English breakfast at the services will keep me going until dinner. Besides, I want to get to The Mill.'

'Might as well keep going then.' He pulled back out onto the road. 'You'll have to direct me.'

The Mill was, naturally enough, an old cotton mill that had been converted into an antiques emporium. Set beside a burbling river, the huge brick building was an imposing reminder of an older, more industrial age. The many white-framed and barred windows on its flat frontage looked out over the Derbyshire countryside like watching eyes.

Victoria had shown him the website but it hadn't quite prepared Finn for the size of the place.

'This whole place is filled with antiques?'

She nodded eagerly. 'Isn't it great?'

'Should have brought more coffee,' he muttered as he followed her towards the entrance.

Inside, Victoria was greeted like an old friend by the owner, much as she had been in London. At least here, there was enough space to spread out and Finn didn't feel as if he was about to be brained by a priceless antique at any moment.

There was a more obviously coherent layout too. He wandered a little way to explore, reassured by signs that read things like *Silver*, *Vintage Toys* and *1960s Furniture*. Still, he didn't wander *too* far. He had a feeling that if he lost Victoria in a place like this, he might never find her again.

'Right. Henrietta's given me a good feel for what we can find here, so let's get started.'

Victoria thrust a piece of paper into his hands. He stared at it for a long moment before realising it was a map of the mill. A large multi-floor map with labels so small he had to squint to read them. 'Just in case. If you get lost, we'll meet by the vintage book section on the first floor, okay?'

'How many floors does this place have?' He turned the map over to find the other side just as full.

'Only five. Plus the outbuildings. Come on!' She bounded off, full of excitement again.

Thinking longingly of the nice cosy pub they'd seen in Castleton, Finn followed.

# CHAPTER SIX

VICTORIA COULD HAVE stayed at The Mill all day. But after three hours exploring all the treasures Henrietta's emporium had to offer, even she was starting to flag—and Finn looked like he was considering flinging himself out of one of the metal-framed windows to escape.

She thought about taking one last look at the silverware room, just in case, but changed her mind when she saw the resigned look on Finn's face.

'You've been very patient.' She patted him on the arm. 'I'm sure Henrietta will have a lolly at the till for you or something, like she does for the little kids whose parents drag them here on the weekends.'

'Ha-ha,' he said without a hint of laughter. 'You know, when I hired you to do this project for me, I didn't imagine having to be so, well, involved in the actual shopping part.'

Victoria shrugged. 'Antiques like you're buying are all unique, and choosing the right one for a space is a matter of taste. I can tell you what fits the right look or era or designer for what was there before. But only you can choose which ones you actually *like*.'

'I don't have to like any of them. As long as they look the part.'

Victoria paused in adding the latest item they were buying to her list for Henrietta to ship down to Clifford House.

'What are you going to do with it, once you've proven your point to your father?'

'That particular sideboard?' He gestured to the heavy wooden furniture between them. 'Probably leave it in the hallway, or wherever it ends up. Come on, we should get going.'

She frowned. He was trying to put her off. And suddenly she was wondering why she hadn't asked these questions weeks ago.

She put her clipboard and list down on the sideboard. 'What are you going to do with Clifford House, Finn? Are you going to live there, take on the estate? Will you sell all the antiques we buy and refurnish it again? Or are you going to sell the house, antiques and all, and move on with your life?'

Across the way, Finn dropped the silver sugar bowl he'd been fiddling with and it clanked across the polished surface of the sideboard. Victoria reached out and righted it while she waited for her answer.

'I guess… I hadn't really thought that far,' Finn admitted. 'I've been so focused on getting this done, I didn't think past showing it all to my father, and winning.'

She shook her head. His obsession with beating his father at his own game could only lead to misery, she was sure of it. But it seemed like something he had to do to move on with his life, and she could understand that. It just couldn't be the end of everything he was hoping to achieve.

'Finn, beating your father isn't winning. If you spend all your money doing up Clifford House like the childhood home you remember, but then don't move on with your life, you won't have won anything at all. You might "beat" him, but you won't *win*.'

'Maybe just beating him is enough.' Finn's smile was crooked, and it hurt her heart to see it.

Victoria sighed. 'We're not going to agree

on this. Come on.' She still had weeks left of working with him on Clifford House to get him to see her point.

As someone who'd had her whole life ripped away from her, she knew how that could leave a person adrift. She sensed that Finn would feel something of that when his big life's goal was achieved—and probably didn't leave him feeling as fulfilled as he'd expected. Then he'd understand what she was trying to tell him.

When she reached the till with her final tally for Henrietta, she was surprised to see one more item placed on the desk, to be added to the order.

A burgundy and white saucer and coffee cup, with tiny green stars on the outside.

'Where did you find that?' she asked Finn.

He shrugged. 'In the nineteen-sixties ceramics section, of course. I figure this way, when we're working late at the cottage together, we can *both* have stylish coffees.'

Victoria rolled her eyes as Henrietta wrapped the cup, a knowing smile on her face. 'What I want right now is dinner.' On cue, her stomach rumbled, making Finn chuckle.

'Leave the rest of this to me,' Henrietta

said. 'You guys get going and enjoy your time here in Derbyshire.'

Outside, night had fallen fast—or at least evening, which started at around early dinnertime in February. Victoria pulled her coat around her as they walked out to the car and hoped that the pub where Finn had booked rooms for them for the night had a roaring fire.

Finn frowned at his phone as he slid into the driver's seat.

'What's up?' she asked when he didn't start the engine.

'Apparently The Mill has reception-blockers in the wall or something. I've just got a full twenty-five emails through, a few texts and… four missed calls from the pub we're staying at tonight.'

Oh. That didn't sound good.

He stabbed at the screen then held the phone up to his ear. Even though it wasn't on speakerphone, Victoria could still clearly hear the receptionist saying, '…been trying to contact you to confirm your reservation for tonight, as our policies clearly state that if you haven't checked in by phone or in person by four p.m. we cannot hold your room any longer.'

Victoria's gaze flicked to the clock on the dashboard. Five forty-five. Oh, that wasn't good.

Not good at all.

In the event, Finn supposed he should be glad they'd only given away *one* of the two rooms he'd booked for the night. But since that meant sharing the remaining room with Victoria...

He was seriously considering spending the night in his car.

The worst thing was it was his own stupid fault.

If he'd looked at his phone at all that afternoon he'd have seen he had no reception. He could have popped outside to check his messages. He couldn't remember another day when he'd gone all afternoon without at least *glancing* at his phone.

But he'd been too caught up in watching Victoria wandering around The Mill, too engrossed in the light in her eyes, the way she'd flitted from object to object and told him everything that mattered about each one, without even reading the labels most of the time.

It was just so hard to concentrate on anything else when she was in the room.

'I am really sorry about this,' he said for what was probably the fifth time as they sat down at a table in the bar area of the pub.

Victoria's smile didn't quite reach her eyes. 'It's okay.'

'I could just drive us straight home tonight if you wanted,' he offered. 'Or find somewhere nice between here and there to stay?'

She placed her hand over his on the table between them. 'Finn, it's fine. We've had a long day, we have a room at a nice pub with a great-looking menu—ooh, pie of the day, I wonder what type it is?—and a nice roaring fire. We're adults, and friends. I think we can share a room for one night without it being a big deal, don't you?'

'Of course we can.' He tried to smile, to relax his shoulders. But in his mind's eye all he could see was the single large double bed in the one room they had to share.

If only there was a sofa, at least…

Victoria held out a menu to him. 'Come on. I'm starving. What are you having?'

The pie of the day turned out to be chicken, ham and leek and served with chips, so they both ordered that. They kept the conversation light—away from issues like the future of Clifford House or his revenge project, or even

Toby and Autumn's baby. In fact, it wasn't until Victoria ordered a third glass of wine with their desserts that he realised she was stalling.

'I could always sleep in the car, you know,' he said.

She jumped at his words, spilling a little wine over her hand. 'What? No. It's fine.'

'I'd just hate for you to have to get drunk to spend the night in the same room as me.' For himself, he'd been nursing his second pint for over an hour. He wasn't a big drinker— a legacy of growing up with a father who liked to share his hatred for the world after a few drinks of an evening—and he knew that Victoria wasn't usually either. Her vice was caffeine, not alcohol. She hadn't even had a second glass after Toby's announcement the night before.

Which meant she had to be really nervous about tonight. He didn't like the idea of her being nervous around him, ever.

'I'm not getting drunk, Finn,' she said with perfect articulation. 'If I was, you should be worried, because I have it on good authority that I snore when I'm drunk.'

Barnaby's authority. The only man who

she'd shared a bed with in over a decade, he was certain.

Of course she was nervous. And he was an arse for not seeing why sooner.

He fumbled for the words to apologise, but before he could find them she'd already moved the conversation on.

'So, Clifford, any women in your life to warn me about *your* snoring right now?' She leered across the table in a way that should be sleazy but was actually faintly hilarious. 'Or who might complain about me sharing your bed tonight?'

'No women,' he said shortly. 'I'm…not interested in romance right now. Got bigger things to focus on. Like the business.'

She snorted in a way he was almost sure she wouldn't have done after only one glass of wine. 'You mean your revenge project. That's the only thing you're thinking about these days, huh?'

It wasn't, not by a long chalk. Because what he mostly found himself thinking about these days, whenever his mind wandered, was *her*.

'I have plenty to think about,' he answered shortly.

Victoria leaned closer across the table, moving her glass of wine safely to one side.

Her hair fell in a dark curtain either side of her pale face, and her eyes shone as she met his gaze. 'You should be thinking about romance, you know. About love.'

He blinked. 'Why on earth would I want to do that?'

'Because it's what's next. Oh, it doesn't have to *actually* be love and marriage and all that if you really don't want to. But you need to fall in love with *something*. Anything. Find something to be passionate about. You get your revenge, you can say goodbye to that whole part of your life, Finn.' Her eyes were dark, her words intense, and he knew she'd been thinking about this since their conversation at The Mill. 'You get to live happily ever after, if you want to. You just need to go out and find it.'

'And is that what you're doing?'

She shrank back. 'I *had* my happy ever after, Finn. I'm not looking for another one.'

'Well, maybe I'm not either.' Finn hoped that might be the end of the conversation.

'But *why* not?' Apparently not.

He sighed. 'Look. If you're asking if there's any great heartbreak in my life, there isn't. I haven't been burned by a scandalous woman, or scarred by a horrible break-up. I'm just not in a place where romance is really on my radar.' That sounded simple enough, right? Nothing to argue with there.

Unless your name was Victoria Blythe. 'I just worry about you. Toby's all settled now and—'

'And you think I should be too.' He shook his head. 'There's more to life than just sex and relationships, you know.'

'I *do* know,' she replied pertly. 'Or else I'm in for a long and boring existence. But for you... Finn, I worry about you being alone. You've been so focused on this revenge project of yours, I don't think you've even thought about what happens next. But when it's over... what are you going to fill that hole with?'

*When it's over.* God, was it possible that it could be, and soon?

Ever since the day in his third year at Oxford, when the news had reached him—via a less than friendly classmate—that his father had sold Clifford House out from under him, Finn had been thinking of ways to get it back. Everything he'd done in his professional and personal life since the age of twenty-one had been focused on this.

He'd never thought past that moment.

But even if he tried now, it was hard to envisage it. Hard to imagine a world where he wasn't consumed by the need to prove to his father that he couldn't beat him. That he was stronger than his father had ever imagined he could be.

Lord Clifford had believed that his son was a no-good degenerate, and had sold almost everything he owned to keep it out of Finn's hands. Now Finn was proving him wrong.

But *after?*

Finn shook his head.

'I'll worry about that when it happens.' He reached for his pint. 'Besides, it's not like I *never* date.'

'Not seriously, according to Toby.'

'Well, no. I'm not looking for anything long-term, so I don't want to lead anyone on.'

'But why not long-term?' Victoria pressed. 'Is it because of your parents? What happened between them? Because you have to know that isn't your fault.'

*Not according to my father.*

It seemed that three glasses of wine turned Victoria into a psychiatrist. And he could already tell she wasn't going to let this go.

Not unless he told her the truth.

Finn contemplated the pint glass in his hand, drained the last of the contents then placed it back down on the table. Yeah, this was probably a big mistake.

But he was going to do it anyway.

'Honestly? I don't look for anything serious because the only woman I've truly wanted for the last fifteen years was you.'

Victoria blinked. And then she blinked again.

'What?'

Maybe she'd already fallen asleep and this was some really weird dream. Otherwise...

Finn chuckled, low and self-deprecating. 'Don't worry. This isn't some epic tragedy of broken dreams or anything. It's just... I had the biggest crush on you, the summer we met.'

'Fifteen years ago.' When she hadn't thought of Finn as anything more than a hanger-on to Barnaby's little brother. Of course, he'd grown up a lot since then... 'Are you really telling me that one crush when you were sixteen has ruined you for love?'

That earned a proper laugh. 'No. I just... I saw what was possible, and I didn't want to settle for anything less.'

'You mean the relationship I had with Barnaby?' Because that she could understand. Her marriage had been a true love fairy tale and she could totally get Finn wanting to wait for something that good.

His gaze slid away from hers. 'Something like that.'

He was lying. He meant *her*. God, he'd had a crush on her the whole time she'd known him and she'd never even realised.

Or had she? There had been moments… times when it was the two of them standing on the outskirts of the family, outsiders together, when she'd wondered why a teenage, then twenty-something, boy would choose to hang out with her instead of doing anything else. She'd put it down to his reluctance to go home, but maybe it had been more than that.

Then there was that almost kiss at the station. The way it had raced through her body, heating her blood… Could it have done that if he hadn't been feeling the same?

And last night. When he'd known, more than Toby even, how she'd be feeling. He'd known where to find her too. And he'd given her exactly what she needed—comfort and understanding.

Suddenly, she saw Finn in a whole new light.

'You know, I feel like the right time to share this information was probably *not* just before we have to share a bed together for the night,' she said.

Finn winced. 'Yeah, sorry about that. I just figured you weren't going to give up until you got to the truth, and this saved some time.'

'That's fair.'

He met her gaze again at last, and it felt as if the barrier behind his eyes was…not gone, but perhaps a little thinner. Enough that she could almost see through to the other side. To the heart of him.

If she wanted to.

'You know you asked me why I didn't visit again, after the funerals?' Finn said.

'Apart from to talk about Toby that one time, yeah.' He'd been so awkward that day. So un-Finn-like. She'd assumed it was the proximity to death and loss that had set him off-kilter.

'This was why.'

She frowned. 'Because of an ancient crush?'

'Because…when you were married to Barnaby, it was sort of okay. I mean, I was never going to do anything about how I felt, obviously, because you were with Barnaby and you loved him and you were both so happy together. It was…safe.'

Oh, now this was starting to make sense.

He'd fixated on her because she was *safe*. Not because she was *her*. He knew he never stood a chance, so never had to do anything about it, but his crush had enabled him to keep other women at a distance for years, because of her. God, the human psyche was complicated. She wasn't sure her psychology A Level was up to this level of denial.

'But after Barnaby was gone...' Finn trailed off, and Victoria put aside her psycho-analysis to meet his gaze. Her heart caught at the torment behind his eyes. 'It just felt so wrong. I felt guilty that I was there to look at you when he wasn't. He was like a big brother to me too, you know. And I just... I'm sorry. I couldn't deal.'

Victoria took his hand across the table. 'You came back, though. You gave me this opportunity, helped me get out of Wishcliffe and look for my future. You're a good friend, Finn.'

His smile wasn't completely convinced. 'A good friend probably wouldn't have been lusting after his friend's wife in the first place.'

'True.' But since he'd never let on, she suspected Barnaby would have forgiven him. She suspected it was far less to do with her than what she represented for Finn, anyway.

And when it came to lusting, she wasn't entirely innocent either.

She dropped his hand as the memory of the night before came back, warming her from the inside out. Just standing close to him had been enough to set her mind to wandering.

How on earth was she going to spend a night in a bed with him, after everything he'd told her?

# CHAPTER SEVEN

FINN STARED AT the large double bed and wondered if there was a mattress in the world big enough for this. What had he been thinking, confessing his ancient crush to Victoria *tonight*?

Well, he knew the answer to that. He hadn't been thinking at all. He'd been watching her in the firelight, amused and touched by the effort she was putting in to figuring him out. And of course she hadn't stood a chance without the fundamental fact that her mere existence had ruined him for other women.

He rather suspected that she'd drawn her own conclusions about his lack of a love life, and they weren't necessarily the same as his. But all the same, the truth was out there now.

And they still had to share a bed together tonight.

'Mind if I use the bathroom first?' Victoria asked, and he nodded his agreement.

He needed a moment alone to think this through.

As the bathroom door locked behind her, Finn sank down to sit on the end of the bed. The room itself was nice enough: pale walls with thick curtains in a deep, warm red, local landscapes on the wall. In the bay window there were two small cocktail chairs—nice to look at, perfectly fine for occasional sitting, he was sure, but no good for sleeping. And there was barely enough floor space either side of the bed for him to stretch out and sleep on the carpet.

No, it would have to be the bed. They were both adults. This would be fine.

Maybe it would even be easier, now it was all out in the open. If he hadn't told her, he'd have spent all night terrified he'd do something in his sleep that would give him away. Now, he didn't need to worry about that. It was a big bed, and he was a grown man. He'd keep to his side, keep his hands to himself and it would be morning before he knew it.

The bathroom door clicked open again and Victoria appeared, dressed in a warm pair of pyjamas with ice-skating penguins on. 'All

yours.' Obviously seeing his smirk at the pyjamas, she looked down at herself and rolled
her eyes. 'What? They're warm. And I wasn't
really expecting anyone else to see them.'

'They're adorable.' And, weirdly, no less
tempting than some lacy and silk confection
would have been.

'Harry bought them for me, his last Christmas,' Victoria said.

'I love them.' Grabbing his wash bag from
his case, along with his own choice in night-
wear—black, comfortable and otherwise
nondescript—he headed for the bathroom.
'You pick a side. I won't be long.'

How many months had it been since he'd
shared a bed with someone for a whole night?
He tried counting back in his mind as he
cleaned his teeth, but once it got over a year
and a half it was just depressing him, so he
stopped.

Finn met his reflection's gaze in the mirror. 'It's just a bed. Just one night. It's going
to be fine.'

When he stepped back into the bedroom
he found Victoria already snuggled up on the
left side of the bed, her phone charging beside her and only the bedside lamps still on.
Cautiously, taking care not to touch her even

a little bit, he slipped under the covers on the other side of the bed.

'Goodnight, Victoria.'

''Night.' The word was slurred, as if she was already half asleep. Obviously that last glass of wine was going to knock her out for the night.

Lying flat on his back, Finn allowed himself a small smile. It really was going to be okay.

At least he thought so until ten minutes later, when Victoria gave a very small, cute snore and rolled over. Right into his waiting arms.

*Hell.*

He was going to hell, and that was all there was to it.

But as she snuggled against his neck Finn had to admit—it might be worth it.

Two weeks later, Victoria still came into consciousness most mornings with the memory of sleeping in Finn's arms fresh in her mind. When she'd awoken and discovered they'd become tangled in the night, she'd slipped out as sneakily as she could and escaped to the bathroom before he woke up and realised what had happened. Which at least meant the morning after hadn't been nearly as awkward as it could have been, her penguin pyjamas notwithstanding.

That should have been the end of it. A funny tale to tell at dinner parties in the future, maybe.

But no. Because she couldn't stop dreaming about how good it had felt to sleep in his arms.

Just sleep! It wasn't as if she even remembered anything except that blissful moment on waking, before she'd realised what it meant.

She'd assumed, the first time she woke up with the memory, that she was thinking about Barnaby. A new way to miss him, to add to all the others she experienced on a daily basis. But no. Her half-asleep mind was very clear on that. Had been even back in that room above the pub in Derbyshire. She might have forgotten, just for a moment, what it meant and why it was bad. But at no point had she thought the arms around her belonged to anybody but Finn Clifford.

It was just as well he'd been busy in London with his actual job for the last two weeks, while she'd been conducting research and investigations from the shop in Wishcliffe, with

Joanne weighing in with a new line of enquiry from time to time. Her only contact with Finn had been the occasional email or phone call to check on progress.

Even those, though, made her remember that night. Those arms.

'Is that another email from Finn?' Joanne had asked the day before as Victoria had sat at the computer—hidden away in the back office.

'How did you know?'

Joanne had cackled at that. 'You're blushing. Again.'

So, yes. Two weeks apart had been great—but it didn't seem to have done any real good.

And now she was meeting him at the Eurostar terminal in St Pancras Station in London, ready to head across the Channel to follow her latest lead on one of the more distinctive Clifford House heirlooms—a painting of Finn's grandmother by a minorly famous artist that had come up for sale at the Drouot auction house in Paris.

'I promise I definitely booked a suite with two bedrooms this time,' Finn said as he greeted her with a kiss on the cheek. 'And I called to double check.'

Victoria forced a smile and hoped she

wasn't blushing at the memory he evoked. 'Good to know.'

They made their way through passport control, picking up coffees while they waited to board. Once settled in their seats on the train, Victoria busied herself studying the auction catalogue on her tablet, while Finn opened his laptop and got on with his own work.

But she couldn't stop her attention from wandering away from her screen and back to his face. His familiar, comforting face—that somehow didn't feel comforting or familiar any more. She scanned his dark brows over bright eyes, the sharp lines of his jaw, the softness of his mouth…

No. Not safe and comforting. If anything, being around Finn these days felt almost dangerous.

Not because of anything he was doing, of course. But because of the feelings that rose up inside her as she watched him.

What was it that had changed? Was it sleeping in his embrace? Or his confession of a long-running crush? Knowing that someone wanted you was a powerful thing. Was it simply that information that was causing the spiral of heat and want inside her? The unbearable need to push his dark hair away from his forehead and kiss him until he forgot all about his damn emails.

She looked away sharply, staring back down at her own screen again. Paris. Antiques. The auction. That was what she was supposed to be thinking about.

Not Finn's arms or lips. Or his smile as he'd told her that, ever since he was sixteen, she was the only woman he'd been thinking of.

She almost scoffed aloud at that. She might not have kept up on *all* the details of Finn's love life over the last fifteen years, but she knew enough from Toby to be sure he hadn't been anything close to celibate.

And still… He'd been thinking of her. And now she was thinking of him.

When Barnaby had been alive it had been almost inconceivable for her to look at another man in that kind of way. Film stars, sure. But actual real life breathing men she knew? No. It just hadn't occurred to her. Barnaby had been more than enough for her.

She'd thought that all her sex drive, her ability to be attracted or aroused by men even, had died with her husband. But now, almost a year and a half after his death, she was faced with the fact that she'd been wrong about that. Very wrong.

Because watching Finn read his emails was somehow the sexiest thing she'd seen all month.

If she was honest with herself, she knew those feelings had started before his confession too. That night in the orchard, for instance. She'd known then. Even when he'd come to her cottage, there'd been an inkling of something, unacknowledged until now.

And when she'd seen him at Clifford House, surrounded by empty rooms and bad memories…she'd wanted to save him. Wanted him to save her, maybe, too. Wasn't that why they were both here?

'If you frown any harder at that tablet, the screen's going to shatter through pure fear,' Finn observed from across the way. He closed his laptop, folding his hands on the top of it and studying her with honest concern. 'What's up?'

*You. The way you keep looking at me. The things I keep thinking when you look at me that way. The fact I can't stop remembering how it felt to lie in your arms…*

'I need more coffee,' she said, pushing her thoughts away.

Finn grinned and got to his feet. 'Of course you do. I'll go see what I can find.'

Victoria watched him make his way down the carriage to the buffet bar, then realised she was staring at his very attractive arse in his suit trousers and sank down into her seat with a groan.

Finn loved Paris. But most of all he loved watching Victoria *love* Paris.

'You've really never been here before?' he asked as she leaned over the balcony of their suite, taking in the view of the Place de la Concorde. The view, he had to admit, was fabulous. But he'd been far happier to see the two bedrooms, as promised, when they'd arrived at the suite. He wasn't sure his self-control could take another night in bed with Victoria without exploding with the need to touch her.

'Half a day on a school trip, twenty years ago. Doesn't count.' She waved a hand, dismissing the whole experience.

'It really doesn't. So, what do you want to see first?'

She spun around, eyes wide. 'We don't have to work? I mean, I know the auction's not until tomorrow, but there are some great antique shops we could visit. Or, if you've got other work to get on with, I could go and find something to do…'

As if he was going to let her experience Paris without him.

'Nope. This afternoon we're just tourists, okay? Grab the guidebook and your comfortable shoes and we'll see what delights we can discover.'

Her wide smile was reward enough. The excited kiss she pressed to his cheek as she ran off to get her things together left a lingering warmth that made him wish, not for the first time, that things were different and they *didn't* need two rooms in their suite.

Paris in February wasn't warm, but they were lucky to have a dry and bright day that made the wide avenues and white stone of the city shine. Map in hand, Victoria led the way, starting with—of course—a coffee from a little bistro off the Place de la Concorde.

'I want to visit the Eiffel Tower,' she said, placing a polished fingernail on the map. 'And we need to at least walk *past* the Louvre, even if we don't have time to go in today.' There was a wistfulness in her voice that made Finn want to promise that he'd bring her here again one day and they'd spend as many hours as she wanted exploring that famous museum. But it wasn't his place, so he held his tongue.

'The Musée d'Orsay would be great too, and I'd like to see Notre-Dame, but actually...' She trailed off.

'What?' he asked, intrigued.

'I'd really like to go to the Pompidou Centre.'

Finn laughed. 'Modern art? You?'

'I can't like old things *and* new things?' Victoria shrugged. 'I'm an art-lover, first and foremost. I love *all* types of art.'

'Then the Pompidou Centre it is.' Finn drained his coffee then reached across to close her map. She'd found one of those pop-up ones at the station, delighted by the simple way it unfolded and refolded after use.

Victoria eyed him with obvious suspicion. 'Why do I feel like you gave in remarkably easily on that?'

He grinned. 'Because you don't know that my favourite crêperie in Paris is right around the corner from the Pompidou Centre.'

Laughing, she followed him out of the café and they began their exploration of the city of love.

Finn had never been a massive fan of modern and contemporary art, but he had to admit that the displays in the Pompidou Centre caught his imagination. Or maybe it was just the engaging way Victoria spoke about them. She had something interesting to say about every piece they saw—even ones that appeared to be nothing more than an over-sized canvas painted blue.

Once or twice, Finn even caught himself imagining a piece—or something similar—hanging on one of the empty walls of Clifford House. Something new, something different.

He shook the thoughts away though, and dragged Victoria out of the gift shop and around the corner for crêpes.

Fortified by more coffee and the thin, delicate pancakes the French excelled in, they headed back out to view more tourist spots on their way back to the hotel. Since Victoria refused to take the subway—'I'll miss vital Paris views underground! Come on, we can walk it!'—Finn estimated they'd walked many miles by the time they returned to their suite.

From the way Victoria collapsed on the sofa, she agreed. 'We don't have to move ever again, do we?'

Finn took the chair opposite her, his aching

feet grateful. 'Depends on if you want dinner tonight or not.'

'I am a little hungry,' she admitted, sitting up straighter. 'Those crêpes were delicious, but not exactly filling.'

'I've got a table booked in an hour,' Finn told her. 'If you want to change. You don't need to, though.' As always, she looked beautiful. Rumpled and exhausted, but beautiful.

'Where?'

'Across town. Don't worry. We'll take a taxi.'

'Oh, well, in that case…' She levered herself off the sofa and headed for her bedroom with en-suite bathroom. 'I'll go take a shower.'

And now all he was going to be able to think about was Victoria, naked and wet, just the other side of that wall. Great.

'I'll just…wait here.' He slid a little farther down in his chair and closed his eyes. Just for a moment.

'Finn? Are you ready? Oh!'

He started awake at the sound of Victoria's voice, blinking in the sudden brightness of the room as she switched on the light. Hell, had he fallen asleep? He couldn't remember the last time he'd taken a nap in the daytime, but Victoria's exploration of the city had clearly tired him out.

'Sorry! I'll just change my shirt.' He rubbed at his eyes, trying to wake up, then looked up at her—and stopped.

She'd changed into a dress—nothing too fancy, just a deep red cocktail dress that clung to her curves before relaxing into a soft, swirling skirt that stopped just above her knees. Her hair was pinned up on the back of her head, leaving her long, pale neck bare down to the neckline of the dress, which dipped just a little lower between her breasts. In her heels, she might be almost as tall as him, if he were standing.

Which he wasn't. Because he was too busy staring.

'Finn?' She pursed her lips—her luscious, red and glossy lips—with obvious concern. 'Are you okay?'

He swallowed and forced himself to loosen his too-tight grip on the arms of the chair. 'Fine. I'll just… Shirt. Yes.'

Stumbling to his feet, he headed for his room with only one thought in his head.

How was he supposed to keep thinking of Victoria as nothing more than a friend and childhood crush when she looked like that?

# CHAPTER EIGHT

THERE WAS SOMETHING in Finn's eyes tonight that she'd never seen before. Or never noticed, at least.

It was there when he emerged from his room, hastily changed into a fresh shirt and his hair damp where he'd smoothed it down. It was there in the taxi, as they sped through Paris at night. She'd taken the opportunity to observe the city lights, but whenever she glanced back he was watching her.

And it was still there now, as he sat across the table from her in the restaurant, candles flickering in their holders between them.

She couldn't put her finger on exactly *what* it was, but it felt…it felt like the candlelight. Too hot to touch but illuminating all the same.

'How's your meal?' Finn asked, but the words were meaningless. His eyes said so much more.

'Delicious,' Victoria replied. She wondered what her eyes were saying, underneath.

The tug she'd felt between them, growing over the last weeks they'd spent together, felt more like a tether tonight. Handcuffs, even. Tying them so closely that she couldn't imagine walking away from this man.

But she had to. Didn't she?

Finn might think his crush was what kept him from seeking true love, but she knew it was far more than that. From what she knew of his parents' relationship, and his unhealthy thirst for revenge, she suspected that he was simply afraid of love—afraid to give it, or afraid he wasn't capable of receiving it.

She hoped that, once he'd put his past with his father behind him, he'd be able to move on and find happiness the way she had. But it wouldn't be with her. She'd already had her shot at a happy ending and, besides, from what he'd said in Derbyshire she knew that the guilt would weigh on him as much as it would on her.

She wouldn't betray her husband's memory, and he wouldn't betray the man who'd been a big brother to him.

But she couldn't help but think… Would Barnaby really want her to be alone for ever?

She was only thirty-three. If she was lucky, she had many, many years to live ahead of her. And while she wasn't looking for another fairy-tale ending, the idea of living them without *any* company left her cold.

A chill that was swept away every time she met Finn's gaze.

They lingered over desserts and coffee, talking about everything and nothing. Victoria purposely stayed away from the sort of conversation they'd shared in Derbyshire—the heart-to-heart that had brought down that wall between them right before they had to sleep in the same bed. Instead, they talked about the things they'd seen that day, and made plans to visit Notre-Dame after the auction in the morning, before they had to catch their train home.

'I've kept the suite until it's time for our train,' Finn told her. 'So we can explore to our hearts' content, and still have time to freshen up and change before we travel.'

'You've thought of everything.' Victoria lifted her gaze away from their shared bubble and took in the emptying restaurant. 'It's late. We should get back.'

'I'll get the bill and ask them to call us a cab.'

She'd walked for miles already that afternoon, and it really *was* getting late. She had an early start and a big day ahead. A taxi was the sensible thing to do.

And yet...

'Is it too far to walk?' she asked.

Finn, who'd turned to attract the attention of a waiter, paused. 'You haven't walked enough already today?'

How could she explain that she just wasn't ready for this night to end, without giving away the thoughts that she really *wasn't* ready for yet?

'I thought the night air might do me good, after all that delicious food.'

Not her best ever excuse, but he seemed to buy it. When the waiter came, he asked only for *'l'addition, s'il vous plait'*, and soon he was settling her coat around her shoulders as they stepped out into the chilly night air.

'You're okay to walk in those?' He nodded towards her high heels, and Victoria laughed.

'Oh, yes. I've run miles in these things before.' She set off ahead of him to prove the point and he hurried a little to catch up, taking her arm. 'Every time we threw any sort of a party at Wishcliffe, I was always chasing around in stupid shoes trying to make sure everything ran smoothly. Got more steps in at those parties than when we'd go out hiking.'

The memory didn't sting as much as usual, something she put down to the wine. Maybe, now Toby was Viscount, Wishcliffe would be filled with the noise of parties again. They'd already done a great job with the Fire Festival back in the autumn, even if the usual Christmas celebrations had been a bit rushed as Toby had been over in Vegas getting his wife back right beforehand.

But she had a feeling there'd be a lot more parties on the horizon, starting with Toby and Autumn's second wedding. And she'd get to sit down in a corner somewhere and enjoy them, rather than having to run the whole thing.

That could be nice.

She could almost feel the hope that had started filling her again rise up, like the first snowdrops after the winter. Paris was preparing to burst into springtime, and so was she. Walking through the darkened streets arm in arm with a handsome man, seeing the Eiffel Tower lit up in the distance, the city lights gleaming just for them.

It felt…romantic. In a way that Victoria was almost done denying.

*Barnaby wouldn't expect me to be alone for ever.*

Maybe she couldn't—wouldn't—find another fairy-tale ending. But that wasn't the same as finding a friend she was attracted to and sharing some moments with them.

She and Barnaby had never visited Paris together. Maybe that was what made it easier. Every memory she found here was a new one, not overlain with the ghosts of her past. Here, it was just her and Finn, enjoying the city together.

'Thank you for tonight. For today. This whole trip, really.' Victoria looked up at him as they approached their hotel. 'It's been… amazing.'

'For me too.' Finn's voice sounded strangely rusty. 'Victoria—'

*'Bonsoir, monsieur et madame.'* A man in the livery of the hotel held the heavy front door open for them, interrupting whatever Finn had been about to say.

She was glad, in a way. She wasn't sure she was ready to hear it.

But she was ready for *something*. Anticipation thrummed in her veins as they caught the elevator up to their suite, along with an elderly couple on the floor above. And as they exited, heading for their rooms, she felt her heartbeat kick up a gear.

Something was going to happen tonight.

The lights in their rooms switched on as Finn slipped his key card into the slot. Victoria kicked off her shoes and bounced on the balls of her feet a little as she stared out at the vision of the Place de la Concorde at night laid out beyond their windows.

She was going to *make* something happen.

'Victoria?'

She spun around at the sound of Finn's voice, and found him watching her with a small frown line between his brows.

And suddenly she knew exactly what she wanted to do.

He was standing right in front of her bedroom door, which made things a lot easier. Smiling at the puzzled look on his face, Victoria stepped closer, reaching up to smooth his brow with her fingers.

Then, with one hand cupping his cheek, she stretched up on tiptoes and kissed him.

Finn froze for a moment, then his hands were on her back, holding her close as she sank into the kiss, letting it overwhelm every one of her senses. He was everywhere around her, his scent, his heat, the touch of him and the taste. The sound as he moaned her name into her mouth…

She pulled away, her face hot. This was too much. She'd thought she was ready, but not for this…this all-encompassing *feeling*.

'Victoria,' he said, as if it was the only word left to him.

She shook her head to cut him off, then braved a wobbly smile. 'Goodnight, Finn.'

The bedroom door shut tight behind her, but she still heard his whispered reply follow her in.

'Goodnight, sweetheart.'

The following morning, as Finn trailed behind Victoria at the famous Drouot Auction House, he was still thinking about that kiss. Victoria, meanwhile, seemed to have decided to ignore it completely.

'What do you think of this?' She motioned towards a carved wooden-framed mirror. 'For the Green Bedroom, maybe?'

Finn thought it was a mirror, and that he looked exhausted in it because he'd been awake all night trying to figure out what that kiss meant. But that probably wasn't what she wanted to hear.

'I thought you had a plan for the pieces we're bidding on today?' he said instead.

Victoria shrugged, a secret smile still lingering around her lips as he studied her reflection. 'I do. But it never hurts to allow for a little…spontaneity.'

She'd moved on to the next item before he could ask if that spontaneity extended to unexpected kisses.

The auction house allowed prospective buyers only a short time to peruse all the items up for sale before they closed to prepare for the auctions themselves. Since the auction was taking place over multiple rooms across two floors, Victoria assured him that strategy was essential.

He hoped she was up to being strategic for the both of them, because his mind was *not* on the game today. He barely even registered that the next item Victoria showed him was the one they were in Paris for in the first place—the oil painting of his own grandmother.

'Here it is,' she said, checking the details again in her catalogue. 'It's up early on in this room, so this is where we'll need to grab a seat as soon as the house reopens. What do you think?'

Finn surveyed the painting dispassionately. Truth be told, he barely remembered his grandmother, except as a glowering old woman who seemed unhappy with the world around her. He wouldn't have remembered the painting either, if it wasn't for the magazine shoot that showed it above the fireplace in the entrance hall.

'It's more flattering than any of the photos I've seen of her,' he said in the end. 'But I still can't imagine why anyone else would want it.'

Victoria shrugged. 'There's a small but growing following for the artist's work. It might not make much, but there'll definitely be other people here after it.'

They didn't want it as badly as he did, though, Finn knew. They'd care about things like the investment opportunity or resale value. He just cared about his father seeing it when he walked into Clifford House again as his guest.

He reckoned that was probably worth more to him than anyone else would be willing to pay.

'Come on.' Victoria was already moving into the next room. 'We haven't got long.'

The painting slipped from his mind almost as soon as it disappeared from sight, as he focused again on Victoria's slender form as she made her way through the rooms of the auction house. She was perfectly assured, completely at home here. While he felt as if he was floundering in quicksand, trying to make sense of it all.

What had she meant by that kiss? Had it simply been a wine-fuelled moment she was trying to forget, while he was tortured by the memory of holding her in his arms, knowing that it might never happen again?

He had to talk to her about it. And soon.

They had two hours after their preview of the pieces before the auction itself started. Finn steered Victoria towards a street café he'd spotted on their way in, hoping for lunch—and some conversation.

Technically, he got both. Over *croque monsieurs* and *frites*, served with strong coffees, of course, Victoria talked endlessly about the auction house, the pieces up for sale, the violinist playing in the street behind them, their plans for the afternoon ahead, what time their train back left tomorrow—everything except the one thing Finn really wanted to talk about.

That kiss.

Finally, he had to break into her endless monologue.

'Victoria… I wanted to ask you—'

She jumped to her feet. 'Look at the time! We'd better get back fast if we want to get a good seat in the auction room we need. Come on!'

And just like that, his chance was gone.

Back at the auction house, they bustled their way through the crowd—Victoria leading with her elbows, he suspected—and got seats she deemed acceptable in the room she wanted. By the time they were settled the room was full and latecomers were plastered against the walls trying to squeeze in.

'Don't worry,' Victoria said, smoothing her skirt as she sat. 'Most of them aren't here for your painting. There's another lot a bit later that's stirred a great deal of interest, apparently.'

How she knew that, he had no idea.

He'd just about resigned himself to the fact that talking about the kiss would have to wait until they were back at the hotel when Victoria turned to him and said, 'Sorry. You wanted to ask me something? Back at the restaurant?'

At the front of the room the auctioneer was taking his position behind the desk.

'Oh, it'll keep, don't worry.'

'No really.' Victoria frowned at him with obvious concern. 'I know I can get a little, well, hyped up on auction days. But that doesn't mean I'm not listening. What's up?'

Surely she *had* to know what he wanted to talk about? Didn't she? Unless last night's kiss meant so little to her that she'd already dismissed it from her memory completely. Or perhaps she assumed he'd never be so uncouth as to bring it up, when she'd obviously rather he forget it.

But which was it? He had to know.

The auctioneer was speaking, now. Finn's French was passable, but nowhere near as good as Victoria's, so he knew he'd have to leave all this to her. But she wasn't listening to the auctioneer. She was looking at him.

'Later,' he said.

'Is it…about last night?'

His heart jumped. 'You mean the fact that you kissed me? Yeah, kind of.'

Somewhere behind them, someone hissed for them to be quiet. Finn ignored them. Didn't they know that this was *important*?

'I'm sorry. Should I not have done?' Victoria's eyes were wide and soft as she looked up at him, but Finn was almost certain he saw a hint of mischief behind them.

The auctioneer was announcing the first lot—not one they were interested in, thankfully.

'You definitely should.' Finn kept his voice to a low murmur, as around them the bidding started.

'Then you think I should do it again?' Victoria asked.

Around them, paddles were flying into the air as bids were cast. The auctioneer's rapid-fire counting was beyond Finn's translation even if he'd been speaking English, he was sure. The whole thing seemed like utter chaos.

Except for the small bubble in the centre, where he sat with Victoria, her words echoing around his head. *Do it again. Do it again. Again. Again...*

Oh, how he wanted her to do it again.

The auctioneer's gavel crashed into the table, making Finn jump, although he tried to hide it.

'Your painting is next,' Victoria said mildly, as she shifted in her seat to face the auctioneer again instead of Finn. 'We should pay attention.'

Behind them, someone grumbled something in French that sounded like agreement with her.

But Finn didn't agree. He knew that the painting was important—the whole reason they'd come to Paris, in fact—but suddenly it had paled into insignificance beside the conversation he was having with Victoria.

'Do you *want* to do it again?' He thought he knew the answer, but he needed to hear it from her own lips to be certain.

'He's starting, Finn,' she murmured back.

'I don't care.'

'You will if I lose this painting.' She raised her paddle as the bidding got underway. Glancing up, Finn saw the auctioneer pointing to her as his fast rattle counting continued.

'I care more about this,' Finn whispered sharply. 'More about us. You and me.'

And, to his surprise, he realised that he meant it.


Victoria looked away from the auctioneer in shock. 'Really?'

'Really.' There was grim determination on Finn's face, as if he'd transferred all his passion for revenge over to her. The single-mindedness in his gaze sent something warm spiralling around her middle.

Up front, the auctioneer called on her and she forced herself to focus, bidding again on the painting of Finn's grandmother, and mentally clocking that they were already fast approaching her highest bid level. Finn hadn't set many limits, but she refused to bankrupt him in the name of revenge. Everything she bought for Clifford House had to be able to hold its worth. That way, when it was over, he could sell them again and not be too much out of pocket—the price of a trip to Paris notwithstanding.

'Victoria.' His voice slipped under her defences, warm and low, like a lazy sunny afternoon.

'After.' Another bid. There was another person bidding via telephone and they seemed determined to take the piece. Victoria gritted her teeth and raised her paddle again. Just a little higher…

'Now,' Finn demanded. 'Do you want to kiss me again?'

The person holding the telephone shook their head, and victory surged through her. The auctioneer called it once, twice, then banged the gavel.

The painting was Finn's.

She turned to him, beaming, and took his face between her hands and kissed him—hard. 'Does that answer your question?' He blinked, apparently unable to form words. 'Come on. There's paperwork to do. And then I think we need to continue this conversation somewhere a little more private, don't you?'

The paperwork—confirming the sale, arranging payment and insurance, not to mention organising to have the piece shipped to Clifford House—took a frustratingly long time. Victoria was aware of Finn fidgeting, shifting from foot to foot and fiddling with the leaflets on the desk the whole time.

She tried to ignore him and focus on the task at hand, but inside she felt just the same.

*'Do you want to kiss me again?'* he'd asked her, and that had been easy to answer. *Of course* she did. How could she not want to experience again the heady passion that had flooded her senses when his lips met hers the night before?

Whether she *should* was a whole different matter. And even now she *had,* the question of what happened next remained, floating in the air between them like a shouted bid.

Finally the paperwork was finished and, by unspoken agreement, they got a taxi straight back to the hotel. There were no other pieces she'd seen at the auction that mattered more than the conversation they needed to have, anyway. The painting was what they'd really come to Paris for, and she'd already won that for him.

Now they could focus on something other than revenge for a while.

*'I care more about this,'* he'd said in the heat of the auction. For a split second he'd cared more about kissing her than about his revenge plan, and Victoria had to admit that felt pretty damn good. Not just for her ego—although it didn't hurt. But because it was the first sign he'd given her that he could think beyond hurting his father to something he actually wanted for himself.

Not that she expected or wanted to be his what came next. Not in the forever way.

The taxi pulled up outside the hotel. Finn paid the driver and they made their way to their suite in silence. They'd had too much of this conversation in public already.

But once they were in the suite Victoria found herself stumbling for the right words to say. The usual euphoria of winning an auction for a piece she really wanted had faded with the paperwork, and even the buzz from kissing Finn again was waning.

All she had left now was reality, and that was far less fun.

She'd had enough of reality, the last year or so. Paris… Paris hadn't felt like reality, so far. It had felt like a dream. A chance to escape everything that came before.

She didn't want that to end.

So maybe…maybe she didn't need words at all.

'So I…' Finn's face was so serious as he shut the door behind them. That didn't fit the fantasy either. 'I guess we need to talk.'

Victoria stepped closer, nodding. 'We probably should.'

'We definitely should,' Finn replied, but his gaze was locked to hers now as she took another step. Nearer, so near she was almost touching him.

'Or…' Victoria murmured. One more step…

'Or?' Finn echoed.

She reached out and ran her hand up his arm, all the way to his cheek, stretching up on her tiptoes until her lips were mere millimetres away from his.

'Or we could skip the talking altogether.'

# CHAPTER NINE

FINN'S BODY AND brain were screaming at him, pulling him in two different ways at once. His body, understandably, wanted to sink into everything she was offering now and ask questions later. It wanted to lift her into his waiting arms and carry her to bed. It wanted to kiss every inch of her perfect skin, to discover her anew.

His brain, however, had other ideas. Annoying, sensible objections to his body's preferred course of action.

'Wait.' His brain forced the word out over his body's objections.

Victoria pulled back, just a little, and he felt the hesitation building in her. He reached out to place his hands on her waist, keeping her close but not touching, near enough that the heat between them couldn't escape entirely.

'I can't tell you how much I want this,' he

said with feeling. 'Really, the words don't exist. But...'

'Why does there always have to be a but?' Victoria muttered. *That's what I'd like to know,* his body added mutinously.

'But I need to know that you really want it to happen,' his brain pressed on, regardless. 'And that you won't regret it afterwards.'

'I won't if you're doing it right,' Victoria said with a smile that heated his blood, and leaned in for another kiss.

He kissed her back, his arms tightening around her as he held her tight against him. After all, even his sensible brain wasn't a bloody saint.

'Bed now?' Victoria asked against his lips, her voice hopeful.

'Just...just promise me we'll still be friends afterwards.' That was all he could really hope for here, he knew that. But even having Victoria in his bed wasn't worth losing the friendship they'd built over the last fifteen years and strengthened while working together the last few weeks.

Victoria stilled in his arms, the heat in her eyes suddenly fading to a more familiar seriousness. 'I promise, Finn.'

He held her gaze, needing to be certain.

And then he gave in to his body and swept her up in his arms, holding her tight as he kissed her long and deep.

He'd worry about everything else tomorrow. Tonight, he had her in his bed, and tomorrow they'd still be friends. That was all he needed to know for now.

The bedroom door swung shut behind them as he laid her down on his bed, still fully clothed. For a long moment, all he could do was stare at her, drink in the image of her there, waiting for him. Committing every detail to memory.

Then she wiggled against the sheets, propping herself up on her elbows, and said, 'Well? Aren't you going to join me?'

His mind had taken a back seat now, and his body was fully in charge. Love and relationships might be beyond him, but *this* he knew how to do.

Kneeling on the edge of the bed, he kissed her once more on the lips before beginning his journey down her body. As his mouth brushed against her cheek, her neck, her collarbone, all his fears about tonight melted away. Because this was where he was meant to be. With her.

He might never have imagined actually

being close enough to touch her, kiss her, before Paris, but still his body seemed to sense exactly what she wanted. Needed. As he unzipped her dress and pushed it down off her shoulders, following the fabric with more kisses, she made tiny noises in the back of her throat that told him he was 'doing it right', as she'd put it.

Finn's body was throbbing with need, but he didn't want to rush any of it. If he only got one night with Victoria, he was going to enjoy every second. So he drank in the sensation of her skin against his mouth, memorised the small moan that tore from her throat as he wrapped his lips around her nipple for the first time, and the way it stiffened under his tongue. He was sure there was no way he'd ever forget the silken feel of her skin against his as she stripped off his shirt and yanked him down to kiss her again. And as he worked his way lower, tugging her dress down over her hips and moving his mouth between her thighs, he knew he'd never forget the way she tasted. The way she writhed against him as he plundered her with his mouth, bringing her all the way to the edge before looking up to meet her eyes.

'Finn.' His name was half entreaty, half

prayer on her lips, and it sent a wave of heat flooding through him. Hands on her thighs, he spread her wider and brought his tongue back to her core, pressing deep until she shook with pleasure.

He stayed where he was until she'd recovered herself, when she reached down and touched his shoulder. 'Up here, now,' she murmured, her voice hoarse. 'I want you inside me.'

Finn wasn't slow to obey. After all, this was his one night.

And he intended to make the most of every moment of it.

Victoria awoke the next morning to the weak spring sunshine through the window of Finn's bedroom. Blinking in the pale light, she took stock of herself, and her situation.

Body—feeling excellent.

Finn—still fast asleep beside her.

Mind—in need of coffee if she had any hope of properly processing everything about last night.

Easing herself out from under the sheets without disturbing an obviously exhausted Finn, she padded through to the main room of the suite, swiping a fluffy bathrobe as she went. The coffee machine was all set up to go, of course, so it was the work of moments to make herself a strong black coffee and carry it out onto the tiny balcony attached to their rooms.

Down below, Paris was already wide awake. Victoria shivered a little in the morning air as she watched Parisians and tourists alike go about their day, oblivious to her observation. As if the world was exactly the same as it had been when she and Finn had walked across the Place de la Concorde on their arrival. When, in truth, everything had changed.

*I slept with Finn Clifford.*

Nope, not enough coffee in her system to deal with that yet.

She drained her cup, then headed back inside. Since there was still no sign of movement from Finn's room, she headed to hers for a quick shower, then dressed in jeans and a jumper that would be comfortable for the Eurostar home. When she emerged, Finn's room was still dark, so she poured another coffee and, better protected against the chill, headed back out to the balcony.

With the first sip of her second cup, her thoughts started to gather—as they always did. Barnaby had often joked that anything he said to her before her second cup of the day simply didn't go in, and he hadn't been entirely wrong.

*Barnaby. I slept with a man who isn't Barnaby.*

And there it was. The thought she'd been avoiding all morning. Longer, even. The thought she'd refused to hear even as Finn was asking her to wait, to be sure, to promise they'd still be friends.

Hands wrapped around the warmth of her coffee cup, Victoria let the guilt rise up in her, and then ebb away again slowly.

It had been over a year. She was only in her early thirties. It was ridiculous to think that she would want to go through the rest of her life without having sex ever again. She'd already accepted that Barnaby wouldn't want that for her either.

So the guilt was there, but it wasn't overpowering, the way it might have been before now. Working with Finn had opened the world up to her again, in ways she hadn't expected. She'd moved out of the safe cocoon of Wishcliffe and her cottage. She'd found a place in the wider world once more.

And a place in Finn's bed, for last night at

least. The residual guilt that remained centred, she was pretty sure, on the fact that it was *Finn* she'd slept with. A man who'd loved her husband like a brother. Who'd had a crush on her when Barnaby was still alive.

But even that she couldn't make stick. She'd never once thought of Finn that way when she was married, and Finn had never let on about his feelings for her either. They hadn't done anything wrong.

So. If she wasn't feeling guilty, what *was* she feeling?

Victoria stretched her legs out in front of her and smiled, feeling like a lazy cat in the sunshine.

She was feeling *good.* As if her body had remembered all the things it was capable of. As if she'd woken up after a really long slumber.

As if she wanted to do it again.

She glanced back over her shoulder into the suite, but there was still no sign of Finn. That was good. That meant she had time to decide what happened next before he got there.

Except…except what happened next was up to him too.

She sighed. Apparently they needed to have that talk after all. At least it had to be easier having it the morning after rather than last night, when all either of them was really thinking about was tearing each other's clothes off.

Sinking a little deeper into her chair, she let herself relive the memories. The feel of his body, bare against hers. His hands, exploring her skin. His lips, following those talented fingers until she was screaming for him. How he felt, moving inside her, so close he was almost a part of her, dragging her closer and closer to the edge until—

'Good morning.'

She started at the low rumble of Finn's voice as he appeared in the doorway. He hesitated there, apparently uncertain even after the promise she'd made. She supposed she *had* slipped out of his bed without waking him. He had reason to feel apprehensive about his reception.

She smiled and held up her cup. 'I needed coffee.'

The tension in his shoulders lessened a little and he returned her smile as he dropped into the chair opposite her. 'Of course you did. But you're…okay?' She heard the question he wasn't asking. *Are* we *okay?*

'Very okay,' she assured him.

The last of the tense lines of his shoulders faded away. 'Good. But we probably do still need to, well…'

'Talk,' she finished for him. 'I know. Just let me grab us some more coffee first.'

Making the coffee didn't take nearly long enough for her to figure out exactly what she wanted to say to him, but at least it allowed her to regroup a little. Thinking serious thoughts was hard when Finn was just *sitting* there, his shirt buttoned up wrong and his hair delightfully ruffled. When she could just drag him back to bed…

But no. He was right. Talk first.

'You asked me to promise yesterday that we'd still be friends this morning.' She handed him his coffee, then took her seat again.

'And are we?' His eyes over his coffee cup were troubled, and she tried to soothe them with a smile.

'Always, Finn. You're part of my family— the Wishcliffe family. I'd never let us do anything that would ruin that for either of us.' But for him most of all, she realised. Given what a disaster his blood family were, Wishcliffe and Toby were all he had. She could never let this become something that made him feel as if he wasn't welcome there.

'That's…good. Okay, good.' Finn, of course, was still on his first cup of coffee. She reckoned detailed emotional insight was probably a good few sips away. Which meant she had to go first with what happened next.

'Last night was…it was wonderful. I don't regret a moment of it.'

'But you don't want it to happen again?' Finn guessed.

Victoria hesitated, surprised by his assumption. *Did* she want it to happen again? Her body was screaming, *Hell, yes!* And, to be honest, her brain wasn't far behind. They'd stumbled into a good thing here; why would they give it up?

Only her heart gave her any pause at all.

'Do *you* want it to happen again?' she asked, while she tried to untangle her heartstrings into a way she could explain to him.

His smile was almost sad. 'Victoria, if I could have last night every night for the rest of my life, I would. But if last night was a one-off, I'd still just be happy to have had one night with you.'

She swallowed an unexpected lump in her throat at his words. *Every night.* That sounded awfully close to the sort of emotions she wasn't thinking about.

No. Finn didn't mean *that*. He just felt, like she did, that the kind of sexual connection they'd discovered between them wasn't something to be ignored. That was all.

But she had to be sure. Which meant putting all her cards on the table. Sealed bids, best offer only.

'The thing is... I like you, Finn. You're my friend, my employer for now, and much more than that. My confidant, maybe. And God knows I want you too. I don't want to give up the kind of incredible night we had last night without a fight. But... I need to be honest about what I can offer you, and what this can be.'

Finn's gaze turned wary. 'Okay. I'm listening.'

'I've done true love and fairy-tale endings. Barnaby was the love of my life, and I'm not looking for anyone to replace him.' He flinched at that, but Victoria knew there was no point not being blunt about these things. If he didn't want what she could offer him, then she'd live. But if she let him believe she could give more, and then broke his heart... she'd never forgive herself.

'I'd never look to take Barnaby's place,' he said softly.

'I know.' And that was why he was such a perfect choice, really. He wouldn't expect more than she could give because he understood why she couldn't give it. 'All I'm saying is… I'd like to enjoy whatever this is between us, while it's there. But I can't go into it if you think there's a chance of it ending up with a white dress and a church. I'm not looking for love, Finn. But companionship, friendship and great sex… I would very much like to share that with you.'

How long had she been out here drinking coffee and thinking about this? Finn had barely been able to remember which city he was in when he'd woken up, all mental and physical powers drained by their incredible night—and afternoon—together. But then, he'd always known that Victoria was better than him at many things, and it seemed that the ability to think in complete sentences after mind-blowing sex and very little sleep was just another one of them.

Taking a sip of his coffee, he tried to work his way through what she was saying. Offering, even.

*Companionship, friendship and great sex.*

Hell, were there really people in the world who wanted more?

Finn had never expected love to walk into his life, not really. And he'd known, even before their first kiss, that Victoria certainly couldn't offer it to him. He was no Barnaby replacement. They'd been clear on that from the start.

But if he were ever going to love anyone, give his heart utterly and completely, it would be to Victoria. Knowing she wouldn't accept it made it easier, in a way. He didn't have to worry about the happy ever afters, or even marriage.

*I can't go into it if you think there's a chance of it ending up with a white dress and a church.*

Well, good. Because he didn't want that either. Marriage in his family *always* ended badly, and he had no reason to think he'd be any different.

In a way, this was like any of a hundred business deals he'd made over the years—which was appropriate, given that he and Victoria had reconnected over work in the first place. Setting the parameters so that neither of them got blindsided later on. No different than him getting her to promise they'd still be friends this morning—and she'd kept that one.

Victoria was asking him to promise that he'd never expect love and marriage from her. And in return she was offering everything he'd ever wanted. Her time, her affection and friendship, and her in his bed. Or him in hers, he wasn't that fussy.

And if there was a part of him that worried that it wouldn't be enough, that ultimately he'd want everything she *couldn't* give, as well as what she could…he pushed it down deep inside himself and ignored it.

He *didn't* want it. And even if he did…if this was all of Victoria he could ever have, it was still more than he'd dreamed of. Still more than he thought he deserved.

Companionship, friendship and great sex with Victoria was worth more than *any* number of happy ever afters with anyone else.

So Finn smiled, feeling the truth of it on his lips. 'I'm not looking for love either. But the rest of it sounds pretty great.'

Something flared behind Victoria's eyes, and ignited an answering heat inside him— one not sated by last night's activities. One he wasn't sure ever could be.

Victoria put down her coffee cup, and Finn

knew exactly what came next. The deal was agreed, now it was time to seal it.

And thankfully this deal didn't involve boring paperwork.

'Starting now?' she suggested. 'Or did you want to visit Notre-Dame or the Musée d'Orsay this morning...?'

'Those antiques have waited this long, I think they can wait a little longer.' Finn took her hand and turned it over, kissing her wrist and grinning as it made her shiver. 'I'm not sure you can.'

As he led her back to the bedroom, Finn gave thanks for late hotel checkouts.

# CHAPTER TEN

TWO WEEKS LATER, Finn sat against the bar in the King's Arms in Wishcliffe and decided that life was pretty damn good.

Across the pub, Victoria was deep in conversation with Lena, the manager, probably telling her all about her latest triumph in tracking down the last essential piece for the Clifford House revenge renovation—a mantel clock that had been presented to one of his ancestors by a prince. Not necessarily a British prince, but still—royalty was royalty. And his father would hate him owning it, which was the most important thing.

It was coming up for auction in London in a week's time, and Finn was already planning how to make the trip special for Victoria. They could stay at his flat, he supposed, but maybe she'd like something fancier. Maybe they could recreate their trip to Paris—only with a suite with *one* bedroom this time.

That was the other thing making life great, of course—his relationship with Victoria. Since Paris, he'd barely gone back to London for longer than a day, returning to her cottage by the sea as often as he could. They spent their days working on buying back the contents of Clifford House, their evenings laughing and chatting about everything and nothing, and their nights…

Well. Finn couldn't think of a more blissful way to spend a night than in bed with Victoria.

They hadn't gone public with their relationship as yet, especially not with Toby and Autumn. Which Finn understood completely. Of course Victoria didn't want to upset her late husband's brother with news of a new romance that wasn't actually going anywhere. Besides, in their loved-up bubble at Wishcliffe House, Finn was pretty sure that Toby and his new wife wouldn't understand, anyway.

It had seemed simple enough when they'd agreed the terms of their relationship that morning in Paris, but when it came to explaining it to others… Finn chose not to. He and Victoria were enjoying each other's company, and why did it have to be anything more complicated than that, anyway?

He'd mostly decided to just stop thinking about it and enjoy life instead. Some days it seemed as if he'd done nothing since the day he'd left university but *think* and plan and scheme. Now, finally, his plans were coming to fruition and he could just enjoy them.

'It's good to see her happy again.'

The voice beside him startled Finn, though he tried not to let it show. He'd been so engrossed in watching Victoria, he hadn't even noticed her boss coming to stand beside him.

'It is,' he agreed. 'Very good.'

Joanne had moved to Wishcliffe village long after he'd left, so he only knew her through the stories Victoria had told him, and a few limited interactions when he'd visited the shop. Plus, of course, the phone call that had led to Victoria working for him in the first place. He really should thank her for that. Maybe flowers. Or an antique vase for putting them in…

'When you asked about her working for you, I wasn't sure it was the right thing,' Joanne said thoughtfully. '*Not* that you gave me much chance to refuse.'

'I'm used to getting what I want,' Finn said. 'Plus her brother-in-law insisted it was a good idea.'

'It was, much to my surprise.' She looked up at Finn and he tried not to flinch under her scrutiny. 'For her, at least.'

'And for me,' Finn insisted. 'My project is almost finished, and I know I'd never have managed it without Victoria. Besides which, it has been good to rebuild our friendship again.'

'Friendship,' Joanne scoffed. 'Is that what the kids are calling it these days?'

How much, exactly, had Victoria told her boss? Finn wasn't sure he wanted to know.

'We're friends,' he said flatly. 'Old friends.'

'Right. Like I couldn't see the difference when the two of you came back from Paris.' Joanne shook her head. 'I might be out of practice at that kind of thing myself, but I know it when I see it.'

'What kind of thing?' Oh, why had he asked that? He *really* did not want to be having this conversation, and he'd just given her licence to continue it.

'A good old-fashioned fling.' She gave him an amused look. 'What, did you think your generation invented sex? We used to have them too, you know. And it's just what she needs. A hot, fun fling to get the awkwardness out of her system. Then, when you're done, I think she'll be ready to move on for real. Find love again.'

Joanne nodded with satisfaction, but Finn felt his heart start to plummet in his chest.

*When you're done. Move on. Find love.*

*Those* were all the things he hadn't been thinking about, while he'd been busy enjoying life.

Victoria had been very clear about what she could offer him, on that balcony in Paris. And he'd accepted her terms eagerly, not least because they matched his own expectations. He knew that love and happy ever afters weren't for him—he was too blackened and embittered by revenge, by his family, by every relationship anyone who shared his blood had ever wrecked and ruined.

But while he knew Victoria was capable of so much more, he hadn't thought about her wanting it. She'd been so definite that she'd had her happy ending and she wasn't looking for another one. What if she just didn't want that *with him?*

He wouldn't blame her. Nobody could seriously look at his lineage—or even his own past—and pick him out as Prince Charming. But while he was happy living in this not-quite-a-relationship when it was all either of them could give, he hadn't honestly thought about what happened next.

What if this was just a stopgap for her? The idea of Victoria moving on with anyone else made him want to vomit. He wanted her to be happy, of course he did. But that didn't stop the urge to burn the world down if she left him to be happy with someone else.

To find another fairy-tale he couldn't give her.

'Uh-oh,' Joanne said beside him in a sing-song voice. 'Somebody's gone and fallen in love, haven't they?'

Finn flinched. 'I don't know what you're talking about.'

'Yes, you do.' She twisted to face him, forcing his gaze away from Victoria and onto her. 'You've gone and fallen in love with her. I can see it in every look you send her way.' Joanne settled back on her heels, smiling up at him. 'Well, this is going to get very interesting.'

Not the word Finn would have chosen.

'If you'll excuse me.' Without waiting for her permission, he stalked across the pub away from Joanne, towards Victoria. He'd take her home—no, not home. His home was Clifford House, and that was still just boxes of antiques and bare walls, despite their best efforts.

He'd take her back to the cottage and he'd make love to her, and he'd cling on to everything they had, even if it wasn't *everything*.

Because it was all he could have, and it would have to be enough. He'd promised them both that.

Victoria woke alone the next morning and smiled at the empty space beside her in the cottage's small double bed. Given the way that Finn slept, curled tight around her, the size of the bed had never really been a problem, but she sometimes thought of the giant bed in that Paris hotel and wondered how having a little more space would feel. Not for sleeping, exactly, but for everything that came before…

Where *was* Finn? She'd assumed he'd got up to fetch her coffee, as he often did in the mornings, but she couldn't hear him pottering around the cottage. And given the diminutive dimensions of the place, it was hard not to hear everything that went on inside its walls.

She lay very still and listened. Nothing.

And definitely no coffee.

Bemused, she got up and dragged on some warm clothes before heading out to the kitchen. The coffee maker was on, which she took as a good sign. As she waited for her first caffeine shot of the day to bubble into her mug, she stared out of the kitchen window at the beach and the waves beyond.

And then she saw it. A head bobbing in the water.

Fear and panic raced through her as she left the coffee behind and, shoving her feet into the boots by the door, raced out the back towards the beach. By the time her boots hit the sand she was running—only slowing when she saw Finn stand up in the shallows, water streaming off his wetsuit. The wetsuit she *knew* he'd brought down to the cottage because he planned to go swimming this morning. He'd told her that and still she'd panicked.

Because as much as she loved the sea, had grown up with it, she'd never consider it safe again. Not after Barnaby and Harry.

The cove here was sheltered, shallow, and not prone to troublesome currents. Finn was a strong swimmer—he'd grown up in these waters along with Toby and Barnaby. There really was nothing to worry about.

She walked more steadily down to the water's edge and she knew the moment that Finn sensed her presence because he spun around to face her, his smile wide. When had he become so attuned to her movements?

'Coming in?' he asked, raising his eyebrows. 'The water's lovely.' A blatant lie in March.

'Bed was lovely too,' she replied. 'But it got a little lonely.'

'You mean there was no one to fetch your coffee.'

'That too.'

He waded out of the waves towards her, and she couldn't help but admire the way the wetsuit clung to every inch of his toned physique. 'You came out to find me instead of coffee? I'm touched.'

'I'm going to get some now, though.' Victoria smiled, not wanting to let on to the moment of panic that had sent her running out there. 'Are you going back in? Or coming with me?'

He stepped closer, still dripping, and she knew before he even grabbed her that she wasn't getting back inside dry. As he hauled her up against his wet self she felt the water seeping through her clothes and couldn't even bring herself to care. Not when he was kissing her, deep and long, as if they'd been separated for months not minutes.

'I think we'd both better go in and get out of these wet clothes. Don't you?' His smile was pure mischief but his eyes were warm with lust and...

And something else.

Something unexpected.

Something she wasn't ready to see. Something she might not ever be ready to see.

And the worst part was, the sight of it still filled her with a terrible joy.

Swallowing, she shoved the feeling down deep inside. It was just the panic of waking alone, of seeing him floating in the sea. Memories messing with her brain, that was all.

'You're right. We'd better get inside.' She forced a smile. 'And naked.'

'I will never argue with that plan. Come on!'

He grabbed her hand and together they raced back towards the cottage, and bed. And while he was still touching her, kissing her, she could ignore all the other feelings that the morning had brought. She just had to focus on where their bodies touched, on the laughter in his voice as he pressed tickly kisses to her side, the heat as he slid home inside her. The rising, rising tightness low in her belly that crested like a tsunami as she fell apart around him.

If she could just focus on the touch between them and forget everything else, things would be fine.

It worked, for a while. But eventually—after a rest, several coffees and breakfast—Finn had to leave, heading back to London for meetings for a few days.

She kissed him goodbye at the door, lingering to wave as his car took the corner and disappeared behind the scratchy seaside hedgerow. Then she let the door clatter shut behind her, poured herself another cup of coffee in her starry cup and sat at the kitchen counter staring at nothing as the thoughts she'd kept at bay all morning flooded back in.

She knew what she'd seen in Finn's eyes on the beach, even if she wasn't ready to admit it to herself—and even if he wouldn't acknowledge it either, or didn't even realise himself.

But, more than that, she knew what had been in her heart that morning when she'd raced out onto the beach to find him.

She hadn't looked at those rolling waves and thought of Barnaby or Harry. She'd looked at the sea and thought of Finn. Searched for Finn.

Her heart had clenched for Finn, the same way it had for her husband and her son.

The guilt swamped her, wave after wave of it, until she was battered down and smoothed over by it, until it felt as if there was nothing else left inside her beyond it.

Because she loved Finn. And that was the biggest betrayal Victoria could imagine.

Finn shifted his weight from foot to foot as he waited outside the London auction house. One week. A whole week since he'd seen Victoria—or even spoken to her properly, as things had been so busy for both of them— and now she was late. He'd hoped they'd have some time together before the auction—to grab lunch at least, or even take a quick trip back to his flat so he could say a *proper* hello. But then she'd messaged to say that she'd been held up at Wishcliffe, and then her train was delayed, and now it seemed to be taking her forever to get across London and the auction would be starting soon.

Up for bids today was the famous Clifford clock, the prize piece he needed to sit on the mantel at the centre of his entrance hall to make maximum impact on his father when he saw it. Finn knew Victoria wouldn't miss this on purpose.

And yet he couldn't help the small niggle at the back of his mind that wondered why she hadn't come up to town last night and stayed with him, or taken him up on his offer to drive back to Wishcliffe yesterday afternoon, so they could travel to London together this morning. All her reasons had seemed perfectly logical at the time, but now they felt more like excuses. Like maybe she was avoiding him.

Unbidden, Joanne's words from the pub, their last night together, came back to him—and he shook them away angrily. He wasn't that stupid. This wasn't love. He hadn't asked Victoria for anything more than she had freely offered him, so she had no reason to pull away.

*Unless she's done with me. Unless she's ready to move on to her next happy ending.*

The thoughts didn't make it any easier to stop fidgeting.

Finally, he saw Victoria's dark hair bobbing through the crowd on the street, and she approached him with a smile that didn't quite reach her eyes.

'You're here!' He reached out to fold her into his arms, dismayed when she stiffened at his touch.

'Sorry I'm so late,' she said, disentangling herself from him. 'Come on, we'd better get inside.'

They found seats in the room where their auction was taking place easily enough, although most other seats filled up around them as the start time drew closer.

'I missed you this week,' Finn said, hating how needy he sounded.

She flashed him a faint smile. 'Well, I'm here now.'

But she wasn't, not really. Not with him. She was a million miles away—avoiding him.

Finn knew that look, that disconnect. It was the same expression he remembered from his mother's face, in the days before she'd left. It was the look his grandmother always had whenever his grandfather was in the building.

And it was the way his father had looked at him his whole life, almost, ever since his mother had left.

At least Victoria didn't have the disgust and disappointment to go with the distance. Not yet, anyway.

'We need to talk,' he said sharply. He

couldn't play the besotted fool any longer. If she was done with him, he needed to know about it. He was a grown man. He could handle it. But he needed to *know*.

'Later,' she murmured as the auctioneer at the front of the room indicated a very familiar-looking clock.

That was what he was here for, where his focus should be. On buying back that piece of his history, the thing that would rub salt into the raw wound he'd given his father by purchasing Clifford House.

And instead he was obsessing about Victoria. Even his sixteen-year-old self would be embarrassed by this.

'Not later,' he ground out. 'Now.'

Bidding started and Victoria didn't even look away from the auctioneer as she replied. 'Later. I need to concentrate on this.'

'I don't care about the damn clock, Victoria.'

'Yes, you do.' She raised her paddle and earned a nod from the auctioneer.

'Not any more.' The admission hurt, but the truth of it was clear in his voice, even to his own ears.

Somehow, over the last couple of months,

she'd come to matter to him so much more than a clock. More than any family heirloom.

More than beating his father at his own game and reclaiming his birth right, even.

For his whole adult life, the only thing that had mattered to him was his revenge. And now the one thing he cared about most was...

Damn. He *had* fallen in love with her.

God, he was such an idiot. And he definitely couldn't let her know.

She bid again on the stupid clock, ignoring him completely.

'Victoria, I'm trying to tell you something important here.'

'Well, don't.' Her words were clipped, her focus on the auctioneer absolute. 'I have to do this, Finn.'

'And I have to talk to you. I have to know what's going on. What's wrong.' How could he fix it if she wouldn't even talk about it?

He knew that she'd never love him, not the way she'd loved Barnaby—and not the way he loved her. But he could live with that. He could live with almost anything if she'd just look at him again the way she had that morning on the beach, before he'd left for London.

What could have gone so wrong in just a week?

One more bid on the clock, and the auctioneer called for any more. If there weren't then the clock was his. One step closer to his revenge.

And he just couldn't care at all.

'Victoria. Please.'

She turned to him at last, but the distance behind her eyes cut deep. 'Finn, just let me do my job, okay?'

'Last chance to bid on this incredible piece!' the auctioneer called. Finn tuned him out.

'As your boss, I'm telling you this is more important than the job,' he said.

Victoria shook her head sadly. 'You're not talking as my boss right now.'

'A no from the lady in the front,' the auctioneer said. 'So, sold to the gentleman in the green jacket!'

'What? No!' Victoria objected, but it was too late. The auctioneer was already moving on to the next item for sale. 'I need to—'

'We lost it, Victoria,' Finn murmured. 'Let it go.'

She shot him a glare. 'Fine. Then there's no need for me to be here any longer.'

Victoria pushed her way out of their row of seats and towards the door, Finn hurrying to follow. But where she was slender enough to slip through gaps between people without too much disruption, his own wider, bulkier frame caused more trouble—and complaints.

By the time he made it out of the room, she was nowhere to be seen. He raced out to the street, only to be confronted with a sea of people—and no sign of the only one he wanted.

He'd lost the clock, and an important piece of his revenge. But he knew that wasn't why his heart was aching.

He'd lost *her* and he had no idea why, or how to get her back.

# CHAPTER ELEVEN

VICTORIA DIDN'T HAVE words to express how much she was dreading today.

Hiding out in the bathroom at Wishcliffe House, she sat on the edge of the tub and counted the reasons.

One. It was Toby and Autumn's wedding day—well, second wedding day really, but since nobody had been invited to the first one, it was the only one that counted. And of course it was being held here at Wishcliffe, in the charming little chapel on the boundary between the estate and the village, just like Victoria and Barnaby's had been, with a party back at the house afterwards. As happy as she was for the couple, reliving her own wedding day only eighteen months after being widowed was…hard.

Two. Autumn had really embraced the spring pastels for her wedding theme, and

Victoria was stuck wearing a pale green dress that made her look sicker than she felt.

Three. Finn was going to be there. In fact, Finn was best man, which made it inevitable that she'd be sat near him and probably have to dance with him, even if he was angry enough with her after London to try to avoid her.

London. God, she'd relived that day in her head so many times over the days since. How she'd managed to screw it up so badly was still a mystery to her, though.

She'd been scared, that was all. Scared to see him again, knowing that she loved him. Guilty as all hell too—*that* hadn't faded since her revelation. And confused. Mostly confused. Because what the hell did she do next?

She couldn't just carry on as she had been—the guilt would bury her. And if Finn felt the way she thought he did…well, the guilt would destroy them both, in the end.

Walking away now might hurt his pride, maybe even dent his heart, but it would leave him free to find someone who could love him back without guilt and pain. Holding onto him when she knew that another happy ending wasn't on the cards for her, that she'd already had her one true love, well. That wasn't fair.

So she'd tried to find a way to let him go. She'd intended to focus on the auction, on doing the job he'd hired her for, and *then* address the personal. But Finn, impatient as ever, had tried to do both at once, and they'd ended up doing neither.

Now here she was. On Toby and Autumn's wedding day, hiding in the bathroom attached to her old room.

'Victoria? Are you ready?' The American twang of Autumn's second bridesmaid, her friend Cindy, rang out outside the door. 'Autumn's almost ready to head down.'

'I'll be right there,' Victoria called back. Then she flushed the toilet for good measure, and heard Cindy shut the bedroom door.

She checked her hair and make-up one last time and took a breath. She just needed one more minute.

In one more minute she'd know whether or not she needed to add a number four to her list of things she was dreading about today. And whether the whole situation with Finn had just grown a whole lot more complicated.

Victoria steeled herself, then looked down at the small white and blue stick on the counter and watched as the word *Pregnant* appeared on the display.

For a moment—a brief, brilliant moment—rising hope filled her. A sense of amazement, after so many losses—not just Barnaby and Harry, but the miscarriages that had come before and after her rainbow baby. And the usual fear too, the worry that this might not last. That another much loved and much wanted baby might not survive inside her. But mostly just the joy that a new life would always bring her.

Until reality came crashing down again.

Her heart stuttered as another wave of guilt and self-loathing washed over her. A baby. When she'd already lost one child she loved more than the whole world itself. Would this baby be a miracle, or another heart-breaking loss?

And, either way, how could it be anything but a betrayal?

She closed her eyes for a second, the sheer volume of emotions swirling around her head and her heart threatening to overwhelm her. But she couldn't afford to be overwhelmed. Not today.

Steeling herself, she opened her eyes. The display still read 'pregnant' as she stashed it at the bottom of the bathroom bin and washed her hands. She forced herself to smile as she met her reflection's gaze in the mirror, but it looked fake, even to her own eyes.

Four. She had to tell Finn Clifford she was expecting his child.

Wishcliffe was filled with flowers.

The house, the driveway of the estate, the village itself—and most especially the little chapel that sat between the village and Wishcliffe House—all bloomed with tulips, daffodils, hyacinths and every other spring flower the locals had been able to pull up and tie a ribbon around. It was making Finn's nose itch.

'I hope none of the guests have hay fever,' he muttered as they waited outside the chapel to greet the people arriving for the service.

That earned him an elbow in the ribs from the groom. 'I think they're lovely,' Toby said. 'They're a sign of how happy everyone is that Autumn and I are getting married.'

'Again.' Of course Finn was proud to stand up as Toby's best man, but as they'd actually been married since that chapel in Vegas in September, the whole rigmarole seemed a little overdone to him.

'Properly this time,' Toby said. 'With everyone here to see.' He looked so delighted at the prospect, even Finn had to smile.

Smiles had been hard to come by over the last week. He hadn't heard a word from Victoria, besides a rather terse email about a delivery of a writing bureau to Clifford House. Whatever the problem was, he didn't want to push her any further away, so he'd waited patiently, figuring that when she'd worked through things in her head she'd come to him. Eventually.

Of course it helped that he knew they'd have to see each other today for the wedding. He was cursing the tradition that the bride was always late, though, as he tried not to fidget outside the church. Autumn had wanted her two bridesmaids with her, to walk down the aisle.

The vicar poked his head out through the heavy wooden doors of the chapel. 'It's time, gentlemen.'

Toby was grinning nervously as they made their way down the aisle—which was absurd since they were *already married,* but Finn didn't comment on it. Instead, he decided to be grateful that Toby was doing all the smiling and being polite to guests, because it meant he didn't have to.

By the time they were at the front of the chapel, though, the memories were coming thick and fast, eclipsing the actual events of the day.

This was the chapel where he'd sat and watched Victoria marry Barnaby, the sheer joy and love on both their faces clear for everyone to see. Where he'd stood up as godfather at Harry's christening.

And where he'd endured Barnaby and Harry's funerals.

If those memories were overwhelming him today, how much worse must they be for Victoria?

'Stop scowling,' Toby muttered to him as the organist switched from the gentle background music to something more commanding, transitioning into the familiar notes of the Wedding March.

It was time.

*I should have found her before this. Held her. Helped her face this day.*

He'd been so focused on what was wrong between the two of them, he hadn't thought until now about how impossibly hard this week must be for her.

The wooden doors began to creak open again and the whole congregation stood and turned. Finn ignored the waiting crowd, focused on that growing gap between the doors.

Then the doors were fully open and all he could see was Victoria, her face pale and a little wan and her shoulders tense.

'God, she's beautiful,' Toby murmured.

'Green's not her colour,' Finn replied, before he realised that Toby was probably talking about his bride, not his sister-in-law.

But Finn couldn't make himself look at Autumn. He couldn't look anywhere but at Victoria.

She looked tired. Worn down. He wanted to step towards her and take her in his arms, but he couldn't—for so many reasons.

Would he ever get to do that again? He didn't know. And he didn't know *why*. The same way he'd never known why his father hated him. It was the not knowing that kept the pain coming, he was sure.

Autumn took the last few steps to the altar and took Toby's arm.

'Ready?' Finn heard his best friend ask softly.

Autumn nodded, then flashed Toby an

impish grin. 'Think you'll be able to remember this one?'

'I'm pretty sure today will be one I'll never forget,' Toby replied. 'I can't wait to see what new memories we can make together.'

God, they were sickeningly sweet. Normally Finn would be nauseated by the whole thing. Today…today he just wanted what they had. Something he'd never even let himself imagine he could have before. Something he'd sworn to Victoria he didn't want.

Autumn sniffed. 'Don't make me cry. We've got the whole service to get through.'

'Just blame it on the flowers,' Toby replied. 'That's what Finn is going to do when he gets tearful.'

Finn did roll his eyes at that. And he turned to pay attention to the service as the vicar started to speak. It was his best friend's wedding. He wasn't going to miss that a second time.

He patted the pocket of his jacket to check he still had the rings. But then he let his mind wander—to the woman standing on the other side of the aisle, behind the bride, putting on a brave face on a day full of painful memories. The woman he loved, even though he shouldn't.

The woman he at least had to try and win back. She wouldn't ever love him the way she'd loved Barnaby, and he'd never be able to give her back the life she'd lost. But he could settle for less than the fairy-tale.

Whatever she was willing to give him, he'd take.

But first he had to get her talking to him again.

Victoria was going to be sick.

There was just no way she was going to make it through this ceremony without vomiting in her tastefully arranged spring flower bouquet and ruining Toby and Autumn's big day.

She wasn't sure if the nausea was because now she knew for sure she was pregnant the morning sickness was catching up with her, or because this place was so full of memories she felt whiplash being here again and revisiting all that love and loss.

Or maybe it was just because Finn was standing at the front of the church, sneaking glances at her as if he wanted to drag her out of there and force her to talk to him.

She made it through the ceremony—just— by focusing on the stained-glass window behind the altar and thinking of nothing but fresh air and her breathing. Most of all, she did not look at Finn. Not even a glance. However much she wanted to.

But then the organ started up again and Toby and Autumn were making their way back up the aisle together, and she had basically checked out of the entire freaking wedding. Worse, now Finn was holding out his arm to her, ready to walk her out.

Biting the inside of her cheek, she took it.

*Breathe in, hold, breathe out. Smile if you can. But mostly just breathe in, hold, breathe out.*

She was going to make it to the door. She was.

The heavily scented air hit her lungs as soon as they stepped outside—sunshine and flowers and pollen and cut grass—and suddenly it was all too much. She wrenched her arm free of Finn's grasp and sprinted around the corner of the chapel, thankful that Autumn had let her wear flats with her long dress.

Out of sight of the crowd of wedding well-wishers, Victoria rested her forehead against the cool stone of the chapel and tried to ride out the latest wave of nausea.

'Victoria?' Finn. Of course he'd followed her. 'Are you okay?'

It took every bit of her strength to turn away from the wall and force a smile. 'Fine. Just…hay fever. Too many flowers.'

'Right.' He didn't look convinced, but at least he wasn't going to contradict her. 'I told Toby they'd be a problem.'

'I'll be right back out in a moment,' Victoria promised, her head swimming. 'I know they'll want to do the photos soon.'

Finn stepped closer, his hands in his pockets, concern in his eyes. 'They will. Victoria—'

'Finn, I can't right now.' If he tried to force a conversation now she was going to throw up on his shoes. 'Whatever you want to talk about…please, it's just going to have to wait.'

'I'm not trying to—Victoria.' He wasn't going away. He was moving closer. This was not the idea. Why couldn't he just leave her alone with her misery and the constant swirl of conflicting emotions? 'I just want to be sure that you're okay. You don't look…well.'

She almost laughed at that. 'I'm fine, Finn.' *Pregnant, but fine.*

She needed to tell him, of course she did. Would he be happy or horrified? She honestly didn't know. But, either way, it sure as hell wasn't what they'd agreed to when they'd started this. They'd have to discuss this, decide what happened next together. But not here, and not now. The nausea would fade again in a while—it always had with Harry. She just had to ride it out.

'I don't think you are.' He reached out to place a hand on her shoulder, his touch gentle. Loving.

She pulled away, spinning around to face him. 'I'm fine. I just need a few minutes. Will you please just leave me—'

The spinning had been a bad idea. Because now the bright spring sunshine was in her eyes, making her head hurt, and her stomach hadn't moved quite as fast as the rest of her and felt as if it was about to complete its revolt at any moment.

But most of all because now she could see Finn—the fear and love on his face. And beyond him, towards the edge of the churchyard, two familiar gravestones that she'd been avoiding since this whole thing began.

*Barnaby. Harry.*

Self-loathing and guilt swirled in her chest while the pregnancy nausea rose, unstoppable this time. She pressed one hand to the stone of the church and held the other out to keep Finn away, bending in the middle as she threw up all over the vicar's carefully planted daffodils.

'Victoria!' Finn grabbed for her and she lurched back out of his reach. Apparently even vomit wasn't enough to drive him away from her.

But she was not having this conversation here, now, like this. Not when she felt so utterly unsettled, so unlike herself. She needed to gather up her defences to tell Finn her news.

So, grabbing her skirts in both hands and praying the dress was still vomit-free, she turned and ran.

The photos, the meal, the toasts…the whole rest of the wedding day passed in a blur for Finn. He didn't even have the mental space to worry about the speech he needed to give about Toby. His whole brain was focused on Victoria.

Victoria, who'd wanted to get away from him so badly she'd been physically sick.

He knew what she'd seen, of course. What had caused such a violent reaction.

Her lover in the same space as the graves of her one true love and their son. It had made his own stomach cramp with guilt when he'd turned and realised.

He knew he shouldn't have followed her, but she'd just looked so...lost. And now he knew for sure how he felt about her, he couldn't just walk away. It was as if there were a thread from his heart to hers and he couldn't do anything but follow it back to her, every time.

Even if she would prefer to snap the thread.

And this metaphor was getting too tortured even for his lovesick brain.

The wedding guests all laughed at something Toby had said in his speech, and Finn tried to smile along as if he'd actually been listening. Autumn stood up beside her husband and took the microphone.

'I can't say enough how thankful I am for how welcome everyone here at Wishcliffe has made me,' she said. Sounded as if they were wrapping up, so Finn felt in his pocket for the notecards he'd made for his own speech. He didn't really need them—he'd had it memorised for weeks, like any important work presentation or similar—but it was always good to have a backup. Toby was probably the only person who'd ever call him a best man, and Finn didn't want to screw it up for him.

'And so it feels right to share our exciting news with you today, while we're all together,' Toby added.

Finn froze, index cards in hand. They were going to announce the pregnancy. His gaze instantly sought out Victoria, remembering that night in the orchard after Autumn and Toby had told them about the baby.

She looked pale but calm. At least until she met his gaze and her skin became tinged with green. As if she might be sick again at any moment.

'In just a few short months, at the end of the summer, we'll become a family of three,' Toby announced, the pride in his voice clear.

As the guests cheered, Finn struggled to look away from Victoria as a memory came rushing back. Of visiting Wishcliffe when Victoria was expecting Harry, and she was unable to keep much more than toast and biscuits down for weeks.

And he knew. He just knew, in that moment, that Victoria was pregnant with his child.

His heart soared for a moment at the very idea, before crashing back down into his stomach as reality hit.

This had to be breaking her heart. They'd

never talked about whether she wanted to have more children, but if she did he knew it wasn't like this. Not when her grief for Harry was still so raw and so deep. And not with a man she didn't, couldn't love.

Finn knew that her guilt over being with another man after Barnaby was only assuaged by the fact that he was someone she'd never have a future with, never seek that happy every after with. And this…well, it had to feel perilously close to what she'd been avoiding from the start.

How long had she known? Was this why she'd pulled away in London? Had she even planned to tell him at all? Finn had so many questions he needed answers to, and he knew he'd have to get Victoria alone, and soon, to ask them.

But a small part of him wanted to pretend that he *didn't* know. To let Victoria hide from him a little longer. Because if he didn't know about the pregnancy, then he didn't have to deal with all the emotions it stirred up in him either. Not yet.

Like the terror of being a *father*. How could he possibly do that? Risk repeating his family's inherited mistakes over and over—raising a child who hated him as much as he hated his own father. As much as his father hated him.

'Finn?' Toby nudged him, and Finn realised that the whole room was waiting for him to give his best man's speech. As if his world hadn't just shifted on its axis into a terrifying, unrecognisable place.

But it was Toby's wedding day, and Toby was the best family he had. He wasn't going to screw up now.

So Finn faked a smile and thanked whatever foresight had prompted him to bring cards for this one, and began his well-rehearsed, light and fun but not *too* embarrassing speech to the Viscount of Wishcliffe and his bride.

But his gaze still flicked back to Victoria every minute or so, to ensure she was still there. Because they *were* going to talk, as soon as this was over.

He might be terrified, but that wouldn't stop him doing the right thing.

Victoria would never love him, he knew that. But he'd offer her anything she wanted to make this situation right. Money, marriage, Clifford House itself.

Because, above all else, Finn Clifford knew two things with a sudden, clarifying certainty.

One, he was never going to love anyone else the way he loved Victoria Blythe.

And two, he was *never* going to repeat his father's mistakes.

# CHAPTER TWELVE

FINN'S SPEECH WAS funny, charming and touching—everything a best man's speech should be. But Victoria had seen him rehearsing it enough times to know that he wasn't giving it his all. In fact, he wasn't focusing on the speech at all, if the way his gaze kept flicking back to her was any indication.

*He knows. He's figured it out.*

She could pretty much pinpoint the moment that he'd worked out what was happening too. She'd watched the colour drain from his face as he'd stared at her while Toby announced their happy news. Finn wasn't an idiot. He knew.

Which was why she wasn't at all surprised when, as soon as the applause following his speech had faded away, he excused himself from the top table and headed straight for her.

'Not here,' she said quickly, and he nodded.

By unspoken agreement they headed out of Wishcliffe House and towards the orchard, which had the benefit of being separated from the rest of the gardens by a wall, and the gate Autumn had installed in it was fairly well hidden. They should be able to avoid being overheard by any roaming guests there.

'Were you going to tell me?' Finn asked, the moment the gate swung shut behind them. His jaw was set, as if he was waiting for her to hit him with a 'no'.

Victoria sighed and rested against the wall. Pregnancy was exhausting at the best of times, and this was anything but that. Finn stood beside her, both of them looking ahead into the trees.

'Of course I was,' she assured him. 'I mean, not necessarily in the middle of Toby's wedding, but yes. I was going to tell you. I only found out myself this morning.'

He jerked around to look at her, surprise clear on his face. Victoria frowned. Why was he surprised? Oh, unless he thought that was why she'd run away in London.

Pity she hadn't thought of that sooner. It could have been a neat excuse.

But no. She owed Finn honesty, as much as anything else.

'Do you know…? What do you want to do?' His voice faltered as he asked, as if he were afraid of the answer. She just didn't know which answer would scare him more. 'Or do you need more time to think? I assumed… Well, I thought you'd known for longer.'

'Since London,' she guessed, and he nodded. 'No. I just took the test this morning. But I already know what I want.'

The answer had come to her easily in the end. Her whole future rolled out in front of her, like a movie trailer. There'd never been any question, for her. After so much loss, how could she do anything but embrace the miracle of new life when it was given to her? As scared as she was, as guilty as she was, she couldn't deny the tiny crack in her fear that was letting the joy in.

'You know I'll support you, whatever you decide. I'm here for you.'

Then why did he look as if he was getting ready to run? Victoria knew that kids had never been in Finn's life plan, mostly because he didn't have one, beyond his revenge on his father. But for someone who'd always been so open, so tactile—always moving, always touching, always smiling… Now, he seemed frozen. Paralysed by her news.

Terrified, even.

'I'm keeping the baby, of course,' she said, and watched his shoulders tense just a little more. Another few words and Toby and Autumn would have a new statue in the orchard instead of a best friend. 'I already lost one child, and this…maybe this is my second chance.'

The child growing inside her hadn't asked for any of this, not even to be born into this world, into this family, into Victoria's own losses. The baby didn't deserve any of the guilt that hung over her like a fog.

If she was lucky enough to be given this second shot at motherhood, then Victoria would do everything she could to do it right. To love her child, keep them safe—and make sure they knew all about the family that had come before them. Their place in the world.

Except this wasn't Barnaby's child she was carrying. And that made a difference.

Finn obviously knew that too.

'Do you want to tell people…do you want them to know the baby is mine?' By people, she assumed he meant Toby most of all. While she was sure that *many* people in Wishcliffe—a notorious hotbed of gossip—would have opinions about her pregnancy, she was equally certain that Toby's was the only one he cared about.

She obviously took too long to reply, because Finn went on. 'You could always claim you'd had Barnaby's sperm frozen or something, that you wanted another baby to keep a piece of him alive. Or something.'

Was that what he'd been thinking while he'd been giving his best man's speech, or had it just come to him now?

'Is that what *you* want?'

His Adam's apple bobbed as he swallowed. 'I want to do whatever will make this easiest for you. Whatever you need.'

'I don't want to lie to my child about who their father is.' She should be outraged at the suggestion, Victoria was sure, but somehow she couldn't blame him for making it. After all, she'd spent their whole relationship making it clear that he was never anything more than a stand-in for the man she'd loved and lost.

She'd never told him that he'd become so much more than that to her. And now it was too late.

Finn gave a stiff nod. 'Okay. Then…do you want to get married? You know, the honourable thing? If…if the child is going to be mine, then they'll inherit Clifford House one day. I wouldn't take that away from them.'

The way his own father had taken it from him. Suddenly, she wondered how much of the tense fight-or-flight vibes Finn was giving off were to do with her and the baby, and how much were to do with Finn's relationship with his own father.

Then the first part of his statement caught up with her. *Married. Again.*

She shuddered, the guilt suddenly overwhelming her again. 'I can't marry you, Finn.'

'No. Of course not.' He sounded as if he'd been crazy to even suggest it. Which he was, but not necessarily for the reasons he thought. She wanted to explain, to tell him how he deserved his own shot at a happy ending, with someone who could love all the things about him that she did—without the guilt and self-loathing that came along with it.

She'd already betrayed Barnaby and Harry's memory by moving on so fast—falling into bed with Finn was one thing, falling in love with him and carrying his baby was a whole different level of betrayal.

'Marrying you, starting a family together like a normal person could…it would feel like I was erasing my past—starting over as if

Barnaby and Harry had never existed. I can't do that.'

'I understand.' His voice was low, rough, and she could hear the pain in it. But she also believed he really did understand. Maybe he was the only person that would. 'So, how do you want to do this?'

'I don't know.' Her body was crumpling into the wall behind her, folding in on itself under the weight of all the decisions she needed to make. 'I think...if we're going to be parents together, I don't think we can be anything else.' That would be too much like replacing the family she'd lost, wouldn't it? She couldn't risk falling deeper in love with Finn, with their lives together, and forgetting what she'd had before. 'Beyond that, can you give me some time? I need to think. Figure it out.'

'Of course.'

He started to push away from the wall and she stopped him, one hand on his arm. He stared down at her fingers as she spoke.

'Being a mother again, after what happened to Harry...it's terrifying to me. But that doesn't mean I don't want it.'

'I know.' He swallowed again, then looked

at her with a smile that didn't go near his eyes. 'I'll be here for you. Whatever you need. As a friend.'

They were the words she wanted to hear. But she could still see the wall they'd put between them, the fear and shame and stiffness. Her heart ached with the loss of what they'd had.

But this was the right thing. It would be better this way.

Hadn't she already learned that in life you never got everything you wanted? Because when you had it, the universe was always waiting to take it away again.

So she wouldn't ask for everything this time. She'd be content with what she could have.

It would just have to be enough.

'We should get back to the wedding,' she said, and Finn nodded.

'I'll be right there,' he said.

With one last look back at him, slumped against the orchard wall, Victoria made her way back towards the house, the wedding and her future.

Alone, except for the tiny life building inside her.

\* \* \*

The front door of Clifford House slammed shut, rattling even the heavy stone walls.

'Finn!' Toby's voice echoed through the empty rooms, making Finn wince as he reached for his mug on the kitchen counter. Looked like his best friend was back from honeymoon then.

The past two weeks had been a weird kind of limbo. Stasis. Waiting for Victoria to decide his future.

But if Toby was here, that meant the waiting was over. She must have told him.

And now Finn had to face the shame of his betrayal of his best friend's dead brother.

'In the kitchen,' he called back, and reached for the new coffee pot to pour a cup for his friend.

'Well. You look even worse than she did.' Toby stood in the doorway and scrutinised him until Finn flinched under his gaze.

'Coffee?' He offered Toby the mug, and he took it. Plain white utilitarian mugs. Nothing like the starburst patterns on the ones he'd bought for Victoria.

He'd been stalking online marketplaces for them ever since. If he and Victoria managed to make it to Christmas as friends, as well as co-parents, he had a whole box of them ready to wrap up and give her.

But that felt like a big if right now.

'Tell me what's wrong with my sister-in-law,' Toby said bluntly, as he dropped into the second camping chair. The other rooms had actual furniture now, thanks to Victoria, but Finn preferred it in the kitchen. It was the one room the previous owners had remodelled completely, so it held no memories of his family, even if it did have some of Victoria.

'What did she tell you?' Finn wasn't about to stumble into unintentionally blowing any secrets Victoria hadn't chosen to share. And from the exasperation in Toby's voice he got the impression that she'd told him a lot less than Finn had expected.

'Next to nothing,' Toby admitted. 'But she looks wrecked and she won't talk to me or Autumn, and you've spent more time with her lately than anyone so I'm betting that you know what's going on.'

Finn had never been any good at lying to his best friend. In fact, he'd never even bothered trying. Still, he didn't trust himself to speak without the whole sorry tale spilling out, so he settled for a curt nod instead.

Toby placed his mug on the small table between them and leant forward, his elbows on his knees and his eyes deadly serious.

'She's my sister, Finn, or as good as. You have to tell me everything.'

Everything.

Finn met his friend's gaze, swallowed, and started talking. Toby deserved to know.

It took less time than he'd imagined to share the bare bones of what had happened between him and Victoria. The hardest part was watching Toby's glare deepen with every word.

By the time they reached the wedding, and Victoria throwing up outside the church, Toby had already leapt to the right conclusion.

'You knocked her up. You got my sister pregnant and then *left her*?'

'No!' Finn replied vehemently. 'Well, not voluntarily.'

'Not voluntarily?' Toby ground out, looking like it was taking all his willpower not to punch Finn. 'Is that in relation to the pregnancy or the leaving?'

'The leaving. Well, both,' he amended. 'I mean, the pregnancy wasn't intentional. But everything else... I offered to marry her, to give her this place, anything she wanted. I only left because she told me she wanted time to think about what happened next. In fact *she* left *me*.'

Not that any of his excuses made him feel any better about it all. If Toby was right, and Victoria really was in a state about all this, then he should be with her. He should be making things better somehow.

Even if he hadn't got the faintest idea where to start.

'How are you going to fix this?' Toby asked, unknowingly echoing Finn's own thoughts.

'I don't know.'

'Well, you'd better figure it out. Fast.' He eyed Finn with suspicion. 'Assuming you love her?'

Finn looked away. 'Of course I do. Have you *met* her?'

'Well, then.' Lurching from his camping chair, Toby began pacing the length of the kitchen. 'What you need is a grand gesture. Something that shows her how you feel!'

'Like you flying to Vegas to chase Autumn down?' Finn guessed.

Toby nodded enthusiastically. 'Exactly! It needs to be big and meaningful. There must be something the two of you have shared that has a secret meaning for you both. I don't want details, but…there's something, right? Something you can use to show her how you feel?'

Finn thought about Paris, or Derbyshire, or Portobello Road. He thought about the coffee cups with stars on sitting in his cupboard, unwrapped.

Then he shook his head.

Toby slumped back into his camping chair. 'There's nothing? Really? You guys have been together for months, behind my back. How can there be nothing you've shared that means something to you both?'

Finn gave him a wry smile. 'There's a million things. Every moment I spent with her… it was magical. That's not the problem.'

'Then what is?'

'She's already had the grand gestures. The fairy-tale perfect life as lady of the manor. She lost it.'

'I remember,' Toby said drily. 'And now she can have it again.'

Finn shook his head. 'She doesn't want that. She doesn't want to start over with me as if the past never happened. I can't take Barnaby's place, and she doesn't want me to. And I don't know… I don't know how to be there for her, how to love her, when we both feel such guilt just being together.'

That was the heart of it, he realised. He wanted Victoria to be happy, to have a life full of joy again, not loss and guilt. And he only seemed to make those things worse.

'You can't make her guilt go away,' Toby said, his voice heavy, obviously thinking of the brother and nephew he'd lost. Finn knew that he was a poor replacement for them too. 'And no, you can't be Barnaby. But you can figure out how to be the best Finn you can be—the best partner for her in this. The man she needs you to be. And Finn?'

He looked up to find his best friend glaring at him again. 'I know.'

Toby said it anyway. 'You'd better bloody find a way to be that man.'

Finn put down his coffee cup and studied the Clifford House kitchen. Then he stood and walked to the door, looking around the white rooms with their stacks of antique furniture, ready to be put in place for the big reveal. For the revenge that he'd waited so many years for.

This was where it had all started for him. It had made him the man he was.

But that wasn't the man Victoria needed right now.

And suddenly he knew exactly what he needed to do to become that.

Grabbing his keys from the bowl by the front door, he called out to Toby, 'Lock up behind you, will you?'

'Where are you going?' Toby asked from the kitchen doorway.

Finn flashed his friend a tight smile. 'To do something I should have done years ago.'

The waves lapped gently against the sand, growing ever closer to the toes of Victoria's trainers. She'd been out here so long the tide had turned, and the afternoon was turning into evening. The spring breeze was chilly, but she'd wrapped up in her coat to ward it off.

There was nowhere else she wanted to be right now.

The sea had always given her comfort, long before it took away her family. Her love.

But now she felt she was coming full circle, she needed the sound of the waves again, building, breaking and cresting anew, the never-ending cycle of tides familiar and meditative as she watched.

Tearing her eyes from the sea, she looked down instead at the photos in her lap. One was a favourite shot of her with Barnaby and Harry, on the beach, just a few months before the accident that stole them from her.

The other, a blurry black, white and grey shot, showed her baby. With her history of previous miscarriages, plus her obvious concern about the pregnancy overall, her GP had been persuaded to refer her for an early scan. So now she had the photographic proof of the life growing inside her.

She'd gone to the scan alone, like she'd done everything alone for the past two weeks. As she had for a year, before Finn asked her to help him with Clifford House. It was only once she was there, with the gel on her belly and the technician pointing out the blur on the screen that was her baby, that she realised that Finn should be there too.

She'd realised something else too, though. A stinging sharp realisation that she hadn't been able to think all the way through to its conclusion there, half naked on the examination table. So she'd tucked it away until she was back here and could consider it properly.

She was carrying her future inside her. She'd known it, of course, since the moment she saw the positive pregnancy test, maybe even before. But now…

Now it felt real, in a way it hadn't before. Now, the ramifications of that were hammering home inside her head. And, like she'd always done before, she'd come to the sea to talk to the one person who'd always helped her make sense of her head before, and the one child who had filled her whole heart— until now.

She was kind of glad there was no one else on the beach to see her, though. Because the only way she could do this was out loud.

'Barnaby…' Her voice sounded rusty, from long minutes sitting in the cold in silence. 'Barn, I've done something. And I think I might have screwed up, and I need to talk to you about it.'

*'Then talk. You know I'll always listen.'* That was what he'd always said, with no judgement, no questions. Just giving her space to work through her thoughts and her problems out loud.

'I'm pregnant,' she said bluntly. 'And the father is Finn Clifford.'

She couldn't even imagine what Barnaby's response to that would be, so she ploughed on regardless.

'We didn't mean for it to happen. But…he came back into my life and he made me feel alive again, for the first time since I lost you. It was fun, and freeing. And I thought that was all it could be. That I was past feeling anything more than that.'

Victoria looked down at the photos in her lap again. At Barnaby's dear, loved face. At Harry, so young and full of life. And at the baby inside her now.

'But I was wrong. Because I fell in love with Finn.' God, it felt good to say it out loud at last. 'I love Finn, and I ran away from him because it felt like a betrayal of you. I pulled away from any suggestion of us being a family together, because it felt like I was forgetting Harry, and you. And I'm still scared about being a mother again, terrified of the idea of moving on alone, without you, but…' She swallowed around the lump in her throat, realising that the salt water on her cheeks had nothing to do with the spray from the sea. 'But I realised today I don't have to do it alone. Do I?'

She'd chosen to be with Finn because she didn't want to be alone for the rest of her life, even if she hadn't expected love to be a part of it. Now it was, could she really throw it away? Keep living in the past, rather than embracing her future?

She owed it to her baby to live the best life possible, to find joy in the world—and love too.

But, more than that, she owed it to herself.

'I'll never forget the love we shared, and I'll never stop loving and missing you. Just like there'll never be a day where I don't think of Harry, don't remember how I love him and miss him too.' She couldn't see the photos any longer, her eyes blurry with tears. 'But I think you'd both want me to keep on living, even if you're not here to see it. I think you'd want me to be happy.'

She deserved to not keep living in the past. She deserved to be happy—and so did Finn.

'He's not you, Barn, but I wouldn't want him to be,' she said. 'Just like this baby won't be Harry. I'm not looking for a replacement for either of you. I'm looking for my future, and it won't look the same as my past. But I think that's okay. I'm not the same person I was then either.'

She pushed herself up to standing, her legs aching from sitting still for too long, the two photos still clutched in her hand.

'I love you both,' she said. 'I always will.

But there's room in my future, and my heart, for more love. And I think you'd want me to go after it.'

With a last look out over the waves, Victoria turned and headed for her little cottage, to figure out what happened next.

# CHAPTER THIRTEEN

IT WASN'T HARD for Finn to find his father in London. He just headed straight for his club.

It seemed archaic that such institutions still existed in the modern city he loved, but if there was an exclusive, patriarchal and outdated club to be part of, of course Lord Clifford had joined it.

It wasn't hard to get admittance either. Finn was famous enough—well, infamous, really—in the same circles that his father moved in to find someone willing to sign him in as a guest, even if he suspected they were only doing it for the amusement factor of seeing Lord Clifford face his notoriously hated heir in public.

Lord Clifford looked up, saw his son and calmly closed his paper, folding it neatly on his lap. Finn's sponsor looked a little disappointed.

'What the hell are you doing here?' Finn's father's voice was strangely even, unbothered, although his words and his eyes showed his displeasure clearly. His fingers, however, trembled just a little as he reached for his ever-present glass of brandy.

Not making a scene had always been Lord Clifford's guiding principle. That was why he hadn't just tried to disinherit Finn through the courts, breaking the entail on the Clifford line legally, rather than just selling it out from under him. Why he'd let Finn's mother leave, but never granted her a divorce. She'd only become free of him in death.

Appearances were everything. And he'd rather appear an aristocrat with no land—of which there were plenty these days—than a man who couldn't control his wife and son.

Finn took a seat opposite him and studied the man who'd raised him with fresh eyes. He'd always been so overbearing, filling Clifford House with the force of his voice, his anger alone. Now, he seemed…smaller. Shrivelled. As if the bitterness he'd harboured for years was consuming him at last.

*Is that how I'd look if I'd never moved on from my revenge plan?*

'Well?' Lord Clifford demanded. 'Not got anything to say? Might as well get out.'

Finn smiled a slow, knowing smile. He'd heard a slight shake in his father's voice—nerves rather than anger now. He didn't want Finn to make a scene.

'I came to tell you that you are going to be a grandfather.'

Lord Clifford scoffed. 'Knocked some girl up, have you? Out of wedlock, of course. You're a disgrace. Just like I always expected. At least they won't get their bastard hands on our family legacy.'

'Because you sold it rather than letting it go to me,' Finn said. 'You despised me that much.' Something crossed his father's eyes, an emotion Finn couldn't quite name but it had a lot in common with hatred, he suspected. 'Or was it my mother you hated? For leaving you, forcing you to bring me up alone, when you were clearly so unsuited to the task?'

Anger flashed across his father's face at the very mention of his wife. 'Have you really not figured it out yet, boy?' His voice was a harsh whisper and, despite the other occupants of the room visibly straining to hear, Finn suspected their conversation was still private.

Unless Finn chose to change that.

For now, he kept playing his father's game. 'Figured what out, Father?'

'That I'm not your bloody father.' He spat the words at him, and Finn froze. 'You really thought your mother was faithful before that whore left me? No. I always knew you couldn't be mine. No child of mine would be so...' He eyed Finn up and down. 'Pathetic.'

*He's not my father. I am not my father.*

'Are you sure? Did you get a DNA test done or did she just tell you?' Suddenly, the truth of his life felt within his grasp. The information that would finally make sense of his childhood.

'Oh, she'd never admit it, of course.' Lord Clifford sat back in his chair, his voice still soft, a sort of manic glee in his smile. As if letting Finn in on his secret was cathartic for him. The ultimate revenge, at last. 'And I wasn't having one of those tests done—the records would get leaked, wouldn't they? But I knew the truth in my bones; I knew it.'

Not for sure, he didn't, Finn realised. There was no proof and Lord Clifford wouldn't have wanted any. That would have led to a scandal. Talk. There'd been enough of that when his mother left, and Finn vividly remembered the rampages his father had gone on, safe from prying eyes in the solitude of Clifford House, whenever there was a news story about her and her new lover.

'But without proof you couldn't disinherit me, right?'

Lord Clifford gave a scratchy chuckle. 'Your mother didn't know that, though. I told her if she tried to contact you after she left, I'd strip you of everything. No title, no money, no house. Nothing.'

'That's why she never came back.' It wasn't a question—he could feel the truth of it. All these years, he'd thought it was because she loved her new life, her new lover, more than her son. But she'd done it for him.

If she hadn't died, maybe he'd have learned sooner—once he became an adult and could seek her out. As it was…his father had hidden this truth from him for so many years.

His father nodded, still smirking. 'I didn't want the talk, of course—it was bad enough after she left, but if they'd known about you, well, the gossips would never have stopped talking. So I kept your shame to myself. But I couldn't have the Clifford family estate and fortune falling into your hands either.'

'So you sold Clifford House and all its con-

tents the moment I was old enough to inherit.'
He could feel his father's self-satisfaction at
what he'd achieved glowing from him like
the fire they sat beside.

Lord Clifford took another gulp of his
brandy, settling in his chair, a victor in his
own mind.

Finn studied his nails, before adding non-
chalantly, 'Of course, you might have missed
the part where I bought it back.'

Lord Clifford spluttered on his brandy.
'What?'

He could have raised his voice, made a
scene, done all the things his father hated.
But Finn didn't need that. He just needed his
father to know the truth.

'I bought Clifford House. I tracked down
the antiques, the heirlooms, and I bought them
all back. Clifford House could be exactly as
it was when my mother left, if I wanted. But
I don't.'

He'd thought he needed to take his father
back to Clifford House, to rub his nose in everything he'd achieved. He'd had thoughts of
a gala, a gilded invitation, and an audience
for his revenge.

But now he realised he didn't need any
of those things. He even kept his voice low

enough to frustrate the eavesdroppers as he went on.

'Maybe I'm your biological son, maybe I'm not. I don't think it really matters. I already know I'm not your son in your heart, and there's not a damn thing I could have done differently to change that.' All those years wasted, thinking if he had just been *better* somehow, maybe his father might have loved him. He couldn't get them back, but he could move on.

*'What comes after your revenge?'* Victoria had asked him. And now he thought he knew.

Letting go.

'Like you'd have done anything differently,' Lord Clifford scoffed. 'This is the way the world works, boy.'

Finn shook his head. 'Not my world. In my world, no possessions—no house, no title, no antiques—matter nearly as much as people do.'

He was still terrified at the prospect of becoming a dad, but he knew for sure that he wouldn't be the same kind of father his own had been. No child deserved that sort of parenting.

Finn pushed his chair back and got to his feet. 'Goodbye, Father.'

And he walked out of the club, past the disappointed eavesdroppers, and went home to find Victoria.

Victoria tucked the photo of Barnaby and Harry back into its frame, then stuck the scan photo to the fridge door with a magnet. She poured herself a cup of coffee in her favourite starry cup and was just staring at her phone, finding the courage to call Finn, when she heard the knock on the door.

Probably Toby again. Or maybe Autumn this time. They'd been checking on her daily since they'd returned from their honeymoon, and she hadn't heard from them today. She was going to have to tell them the truth soon. But she needed to talk to Finn first.

She crossed to the door and opened it, her heart jumping as she found Finn Clifford standing on her doorstep.

'Hi.' His hair was scruffed up, as if he'd been running his hands through it in the car, and his suit was rumpled. But the look in his eye, the fervent way his gaze ran across her, as if checking for changes, told her he'd missed her as much as she'd missed him.

'Can I come in?' he asked.

Nodding, she stepped out of the way to let him in. 'I'm glad you're here.'

He gave her a relieved smile, some of the tension dropping from his shoulders. 'Yeah? Good. I wasn't sure…after everything.'

She'd made him think she didn't want him around, when in fact the exact opposite was true. It had just taken her a while to see it.

Victoria headed for the fridge and took down the scan photo again. 'I was about to call you. I wanted to show you this.'

Finn's fingers trembled slightly as he took the small square of paper from her. 'This is our baby?'

Warmth filled her at the awe in his voice. 'Our baby,' she agreed.

He stared at the scan for a long moment before saying, 'I went to see my father today.'

She reached for her coffee. 'How did that go?' She wasn't one hundred per cent sure she wanted to know. Not if it meant that Finn was still focused on his revenge plan above all else.

'He believes I'm not biologically his,' he said baldly, and Victoria looked up in surprise. She'd heard plenty of rumours about the Clifford family and their animosities, but never that. 'He has no proof, and my mother denied it, but he's sure. That's why he hated me, my whole childhood. Why he took away my birth right and sold it, rather than let it fall into my hands when he died. Because he wanted to hurt me, and my mother, and still keep face. It was all about him—not me. Not really. There was nothing I could have done to change any of it.'

Victoria smiled softly. She'd never really doubted that Finn's father was at fault, but it was nice to see that now *Finn* believed it too. 'Did you tell him about Clifford House? About the antiques.'

His response was a slow nod. 'I told him. But…it doesn't matter any more, not really. I don't need him to come here and see it. I don't need to prove anything to him.'

'Because he's not really your father?'

'No. Because he's not worth it.' Finn took a long, shuddering breath, placed the scan on the kitchen counter, then reached out to take her hands. 'I realised that before—that horrible day at the auction in London, I think—but it was only today that it fully sank in what that means.'

'What does it mean?' She hadn't meant to whisper, but the words came out that way anyway. As if the whole future of the universe hung on his next words.

'It means... I was living in the past. Even though I thought I'd grown up, moved on and found my own life, inside I was still locked up at Clifford House, not understanding why my father hated me, why my mother left and never came back. I couldn't see a future that didn't repeat my parents' mistakes.

'I thought that buying back Clifford House would prove something—that I was worthy, perhaps, or that my father had been wrong about me. But when I got there...it was so empty. So devoid of any of the things I wanted in my life, and all it did was remind me of how wretched my existence had been there. And I kept on trying to fill it anyway, because I just didn't know what else to do. Until you.'

'Me?'

'You. You helped me fill the damn house—even though you thought I was a fool for doing it.'

Victoria winced. 'Ah, you noticed that, did you?'

'You weren't subtle about it, sweetheart.' Finn was still smiling though, so she figured it was okay. 'You showed me that I needed to be thinking about the future, not the past. And for me…for me, you *are* my future. You and our child, however you want me to be a part of that. And I'm hoping—' He broke off, as if he was afraid to say the words.

'What are you hoping, Finn?' Because she really hoped it was the same thing that she was hoping.

'I know I can't be Barnaby for you. I could never replace the love of your life, and I wouldn't try. But I love you, you see—more than I ever imagined I could love anyone. More than I thought I was capable of. So I'm hoping there might be a corner of your heart left for me. That you might want to build that new future together, as a family. Because I want more than just visitation rights and co-parenting. I want to do so much better than my own parents. And I want to do it with you, because you're the best person I know.'

Victoria looked up into his hopeful, helpless, scared eyes and smiled as the rightness of it all washed through her.

'Okay.'

Finn blinked. 'Okay?'

He was offering her his whole heart, and asking for her future in return, and all she said was *okay*?

Reaching up, Victoria placed her hand against his cheek and smiled again, the soft, sweet smile he loved so much. 'Let me get you a coffee,' she said. 'You're not the only one who had an epiphany today, you know.'

They settled together on the sofa in the lounge, matching starry coffee cups in hand. It felt domestic. It felt like home.

'When I went for the scan... I went alone, because I've got so used to doing things alone over the past year or so. But when I got there I realised... I wanted you with me.'

'You know I'd have been there if you'd asked, right?' Finn said.

She nodded. 'And next time I hope you will. But...' She took a deep breath, and he knew that whatever came next wouldn't be easy for her—but it would be important.

He put down his coffee cup and listened.

'That day in London...that wasn't the start of it. Me pulling away, I mean. It was that last day you were here, and you went for a swim on the beach. Do you remember?'

'Of course I remember.' Before now, it was the last time she'd looked at him like he mattered to her.

'I realised two things that day. First, that you were in love with me.'

He barked a laugh. 'You knew before I did, then.'

She gave him a look that seemed to say *Are you honestly surprised by this?* And when he thought about it, he wasn't really, so he let her carry on.

'Second, I realised that I loved you too. And it terrified me.'

Finn thought his heart might just stop in shock. 'You *loved* me? Then why—?'

'You know why.'

'Barnaby. And Harry.'

She nodded. 'It felt like I was betraying them. Erasing my past to build a future with you.'

'And do you…do you still feel that way?' God, he hoped not. Because if anything could dampen this small flame of hope that was burning inside him, it would be that.

'You said you knew I could never love you as much as I loved Barnaby,' she said, which wasn't an answer at all.

'And I'd never expect you to,' he added quickly. 'What you and Barnaby had, that was once in a lifetime. I'm not going to try to match up to that.'

'That's the point. You don't need to.' Placing her cup of coffee on the table, she smiled at him. 'That's what I realised, you see. It's not that I can't love you as *much* as Barnaby, the same way I'm not worried that I won't love the new baby as much as I loved Harry. I'll *always* love the ones I've lost. But that doesn't mean I can't love you and the new baby just as much, in a new way. Because I'm a new person now too.'

It was so much more than he'd ever hoped for, Finn couldn't find the words to tell her.

She seemed to understand, though, because she took his hand in hers and held it to her heart. 'Grief doesn't mean you lose that part of your heart. I get that now. But just like with having another child, your heart keeps growing, expanding, to make room to love new things, and new people. Like I love you.'

He didn't need words anyway, Finn decided as he swooped in to kiss her, pouring all his love and hope into the kiss.

'So we'll be a family?' He pulled away just enough to speak, resting his forehead against hers.

'A family. Yes.' She gave an apologetic smile. 'I haven't thought it all through yet— the details, I mean. How it will all work—'

'Doesn't matter,' Finn said fiercely. 'As

long as I love you and you love me—we can figure out everything else later.'

And then he kissed her again. Because the one thing he knew for sure was, whenever, wherever Victoria was with him, he was home.

# EPILOGUE

CLIFFORD HOUSE WAS full.

Full of people, full of music, full of chatter and full of love, spilling out into the gardens and the warm summer evening air.

What it *wasn't* full of was antiques that Victoria was pretty sure Finn had never even liked in the first place. Oh, they'd kept some pieces—the painting of his grandmother, for instance, and the huge dining table that let them invite all their friends and family around for dinner at the same time. But they'd supplemented them with items they really loved—new buys next to antiques, thrift store finds next to upcycled objects. They'd built a home that felt like *them,* and Victoria was thrilled they got to share it with the people they loved tonight, at their housewarming party.

Most of the people at the party she'd known

for years, but there was one newcomer—a darkly attractive, brooding sort of man—who was hovering on the outskirts of the festivities. While Victoria had watched, she'd seen a few people try to engage him in conversation, before moving on when their efforts were met with what seemed like a polite but indifferent rebuff.

Everyone in the room knew who he was, though. Hell, everyone in the *town* and probably two towns over knew he was Max Blythe. The illegitimate older brother of the Viscount of Wishcliffe, Toby Blythe. The man who would have been her brother-in-law, if Barnaby had lived.

Ever since Toby had announced that Max would be taking over the manor house at Wells-on-Water, just across from Wishcliffe, the whole area had been abuzz with the gossip. And now he was here…well, Victoria didn't see the gossip dying down any time soon.

As hostess, though, she definitely had a duty to go and say hello. Toby had introduced them at one of his and Autumn's Sunday dinners at Wishcliffe the week before, so at least they'd got that awkward first meeting out of the way already.

She made her way across the ballroom, her ever-growing belly clearing a path. She was sure she hadn't been this big at five months with Harry. Her only consolation was that, at eight months along, Autumn was even bigger. That and the fact that Finn really seemed to like her pregnant...

'Victoria,' Max said as she reached him. 'Thank you for inviting me tonight. You have a lovely home.'

She inclined her head to accept the compliment. 'Thank you for coming. I'm sorry my home is filled with such gossips.'

He chuckled at that, which she liked. At least he didn't seem to be taking his notoriety too seriously.

'Why don't I find someone to introduce you to who probably won't ask you too many invasive questions?' she suggested.

'That would be nice,' Max replied.

Victoria scanned the room until her gaze landed on a familiar blonde across the way. 'Perfect.' Taking Max's arm, she led him towards her target. 'Max, let me introduce Lena Phillips. She's the manager of the King's Arms pub in town.'

Lena turned, her perfectly arched eyebrows raised in surprise. 'Max Blythe. Really.'

'Apparently so,' he said. 'Hello, Lena.'

Victoria looked between them, sure she was missing something here, but completely unsure what.

But, before she could ask, Finn appeared at her side. 'Excuse me, Max, Lena, I just need to borrow my fiancée for a moment.'

'Borrow me?' Victoria objected as he steered her out of the ballroom and towards his study. 'What am I? A phone charger?'

'You are the light of my life, my future and the mother of my child,' Finn pronounced. 'And I need to show you something.'

'It had better be something good,' she grumbled. 'I was just about to figure out what the deal is with Max. I think he and Lena might have history.'

'It *is* good. Look.' He motioned towards the computer screen on his desk, and Victoria cooed at the sight of the most darling carved antique crib.

'Oh, that would be *perfect* in the nursery!'

'I know!' Finn moved behind her, his arms wrapped around her growing belly, his breath warm against her ear. 'The only catch is, we need to go to Paris to buy it.'

'I have very fond memories of Paris,' Victoria said.

'Mmm, me too.' He kissed her ear. 'It's our place, right?'

Victoria turned in his arms and smiled up at him. 'You're my place. You're my home now.'

And as she kissed him she knew that her future—and her heart—were safe in his arms.

\* \* \* \* \*

*If you missed the previous story in*
*The Heirs of Wishcliffe trilogy*
*check out* Vegas Wedding to Forever

*And if you enjoyed this story, check out*
*these other great reads from*
*Sophie Pembroke*

The Princess and the Rebel Billionaire
A Midnight Kiss to Seal the Deal
Awakening His Shy Cinderella

*Available now!*